Gunman's Tally

SELECTED FICTION WORKS BY
L. RON HUBBARD

FANTASY
The Case of the Friendly Corpse
Death's Deputy
Fear
The Ghoul
The Indigestible Triton
Slaves of Sleep & The Masters of Sleep
Typewriter in the Sky
The Ultimate Adventure

SCIENCE FICTION
Battlefield Earth
The Conquest of Space
The End Is Not Yet
Final Blackout
The Kilkenny Cats
The Kingslayer
The Mission Earth Dekalogy*
Ole Doc Methuselah
To the Stars

ADVENTURE
The Hell Job series

WESTERN
Buckskin Brigades
Empty Saddles
Guns of Mark Jardine
Hot Lead Payoff

A full list of L. Ron Hubbard's
novellas and short stories is provided at the back.

*Dekalogy—a group of ten volumes

L. RON HUBBARD

Gunman's
Tally

GALAXY
PRESS

Published by
Galaxy Press, LLC
7051 Hollywood Boulevard, Suite 200
Hollywood, CA 90028

Printed in the United States of America.

ISBN-10 1-59212-275-2
ISBN-13 978-1-59212-275-2

Library of Congress Control Number: 2007903606

Contents

Stories from Pulp Fiction's Golden Age

A ND it *was* a golden age.
The 1930s and 1940s were a vibrant, seminal time for a gigantic audience of eager readers, probably the largest per capita audience of readers in American history. The magazine racks were chock-full of publications with ragged trims, garish cover art, cheap brown pulp paper, low cover prices—and the most excitement you could hold in your hands.

"Pulp" magazines, named for their rough-cut, pulpwood paper, were a vehicle for more amazing tales than Scheherazade could have told in a million and one nights. Set apart from higher-class "slick" magazines, printed on fancy glossy paper with quality artwork and superior production values, the pulps were for the "rest of us," adventure story after adventure story for people who liked to *read*. Pulp fiction authors were no-holds-barred entertainers—real storytellers. They were more interested in a thrilling plot twist, a horrific villain or a white-knuckle adventure than they were in lavish prose or convoluted metaphors.

The sheer volume of tales released during this wondrous golden age remains unmatched in any other period of literary history—hundreds of thousands of published stories in over nine hundred different magazines. Some titles lasted only an issue or two; many magazines succumbed to paper shortages during World War II, while others endured for decades yet. Pulp fiction remains as a treasure trove of stories you can read, stories you can love, stories you can remember. The stories were driven by plot and character, with grand heroes, terrible villains, beautiful damsels (often in distress), diabolical plots, amazing places, breathless romances. The readers wanted to be taken beyond the mundane, to live adventures far removed from their ordinary lives—and the pulps rarely failed to deliver.

In that regard, pulp fiction stands in the tradition of all memorable literature. For as history has shown, good stories are much more than fancy prose. William Shakespeare, Charles Dickens, Jules Verne, Alexandre Dumas—many of the greatest literary figures wrote their fiction for the readers, not simply literary colleagues and academic admirers. And writers for pulp magazines were no exception. These publications reached an audience that dwarfed the circulations of today's short story magazines. Issues of the pulps were scooped up and read by over thirty million avid readers each month.

Because pulp fiction writers were often paid no more than a cent a word, they had to become prolific or starve. They also had to write aggressively. As Richard Kyle, publisher and editor of *Argosy*, the first and most long-lived of the pulps, so pointedly explained: "The pulp magazine writers, the best of them, worked for markets that did not write for critics or attempt to satisfy timid advertisers. Not having to answer to anyone other than their readers, they wrote about human beings on the edges of the unknown, in those new lands the future would explore. They wrote for what we would become, not for what we had already been."

Some of the more lasting names that graced the pulps include H. P. Lovecraft, Edgar Rice Burroughs, Robert E. Howard, Max Brand, Louis L'Amour, Elmore Leonard, Dashiell Hammett, Raymond Chandler, Erle Stanley Gardner, John D. MacDonald, Ray Bradbury, Isaac Asimov, Robert Heinlein—and, of course, L. Ron Hubbard.

In a word, he was among the most prolific and popular writers of the era. He was also the most enduring—hence this series—and certainly among the most legendary. It all began only months after he first tried his hand at fiction, with L. Ron Hubbard tales appearing in *Thrilling Adventures, Argosy, Five-Novels Monthly, Detective Fiction Weekly, Top-Notch, Texas Ranger, War Birds, Western Stories,* even *Romantic Range.* He could write on any subject, in any genre, from jungle explorers to deep-sea divers, from G-men and gangsters, cowboys and flying aces to mountain climbers, hard-boiled detectives and spies. But he really began to shine when he turned his talent to science fiction and fantasy of which he authored nearly fifty novels or novelettes to forever change the shape of those genres.

Following in the tradition of such famed authors as Herman Melville, Mark Twain, Jack London and Ernest Hemingway, Ron Hubbard actually lived adventures that his own characters would have admired—as an ethnologist among primitive tribes, as prospector and engineer in hostile climes, as a captain of vessels on four oceans. He even wrote a series of articles for *Argosy*, called "Hell Job," in which he lived and told of the most dangerous professions a man could put his hand to.

Finally, and just for good measure, he was also an accomplished photographer, artist, filmmaker, musician and educator. But he was first and foremost a *writer*, and that's the L. Ron Hubbard we come to know through the pages of this volume.

This library of Stories from the Golden Age presents the best of L. Ron Hubbard's fiction from the heyday of storytelling, the Golden Age of the pulp magazines. In these eighty volumes, readers are treated to a full banquet of 153 stories, a kaleidoscope of tales representing every imaginable genre: science fiction, fantasy, western, mystery, thriller, horror, even romance—action of all kinds and in all places.

Because the pulps themselves were printed on such inexpensive paper with high acid content, issues were not meant to endure. As the years go by, the original issues of every pulp from *Argosy* through *Zeppelin Stories* continue crumbling into brittle, brown dust. This library preserves the L. Ron Hubbard tales from that era, presented with a distinctive look that brings back the nostalgic flavor of those times.

L. Ron Hubbard's Stories from the Golden Age has something for every taste, every reader. These tales will return you to a time when fiction was good clean entertainment and the most fun a kid could have on a rainy afternoon or the best thing an adult could enjoy after a long day at work.

Pick up a volume, and remember what reading is supposed to be all about. Remember curling up with a *great story*.

—Kevin J. Anderson

KEVIN J. ANDERSON *is the author of more than ninety critically acclaimed works of speculative fiction, including* The Saga of Seven Suns, *the continuation of the* Dune Chronicles *with Brian Herbert, and his* New York Times *bestselling novelization of L. Ron Hubbard's* Ai! Pedrito!

Gunman's Tally

Chapter One

THE two horsemen streaked out of a patch of sage, one a length ahead of the other, dashed down the edge of a dry gulch and came streaming up the far side, leaving long curls of hot desert dust to unwind against the brittle heat of the day.

The man in the lead rode with teeth bared to the withering blast of his speed. His chin thong had bitten deep against his cheeks with the pressure of the wind against his stiff, straight-brimmed hat.

He loved his gray, that man, and yet his whip arm was never still as quirt rose and fell against the foaming flanks of his stretching mount.

The four-point rowels had left their many bright dots of red in the racing gray's flanks and jabbed now across the open to leave many more.

The alkali dust was in the rider's throat but he did not taste it. It was in his eyes but did not dim the fierce heat of his merciless glance.

He saw nothing of the red buttes before them, felt nothing of the sun's scorching, dehydrating ferocity. He was Easy Bill, on his way to Red Butte and to death.

He heard nothing of his companion's shouts. He had not yet realized that his companion was there.

Easy Bill Gates had forgotten his friend—he who would need so many friends in the short future.

But Jimmy Langman had not forgotten Easy Bill and he spurred his tortured sorrel through the melting-hot day, trying to keep in sight of the gray. Smiling Jimmy Langman was not smiling at this hour. He knew he would be needed, he would gladly have substituted himself. He had to keep up with Easy Bill.

"For God's sake, pull in!"

Smiling Jimmy's voice was thin and the racing wind whipped it back in his face with the dry sting of the alkali.

"You're killing your bronc!"

But Smiling Jimmy might as well have pleaded with the Joshua trees on the far horizon as with Easy Bill Gates that day.

The gray's heart was great, his stride was long. His speed had fattened Easy Bill's purse half a hundred times. But Easy Bill thought Buster, the gray, crawled that afternoon.

The ride was eternity. The way was infinity.

But Easy Bill would have ridden hellbent for China to meet Fanner Marsten. And Fanner Marsten was in Red Butte, a gun on each hip, a smile on his twisted face, waiting and watching for Easy Bill.

Jimmy Langman withheld his quirt to the last. Easy Bill flashed down a curving road strewn with black, smoking-hot lava stones, far in advance now.

Jimmy Langman let his quirt fall.

"Sorry, Mike," he told his sorrel and struck again.

"Sorry, Mike."

He dug his spurs.

"You understand, Mike. We got to be there with him."

The sorrel rushed down the stone-strewn road, breasting Easy Bill's dust, laying a smoke screen of his own.

Hoofs rolling, faster and faster. Hoofs thundering, louder and louder.

Fanner Marsten was waiting with a gun on each hip. Waiting for Easy Bill Gates.

Far off across the bleak waste, broiling between the coals of red canyon walls, Red Butte came into sight, twisted and shivering and squirming with the barrage of heat waves which shot skyward like a billion glass snakes toward the smoking bullion of the sun.

The gray was belly deep in the dust, reaching, reaching, reaching. The sorrel stretched out, shiny and white with lather, keeping up to the snare-drum rattle of Buster's racing hoofs.

"Take him, boy," pleaded Smiling Jimmy.

"Take him, boy."

"We got to be there when they draw."

Since the first instant he had glimpsed Red Butte writhing on its rack of heat in the canyon walls, Easy Bill had not once taken his eyes away from the miserable collection of weary, weathered buildings.

Fanner Marsten was waiting there with a gun on each hip and a smile on his twisted face.

Easy Bill's features were frozen by a glue of dust and sweat and hate. In all this withering, frying heat, his brain was frozen, a cake of ice, congealed around one thought—Fanner Marsten must pay!

Thundering hoofs, louder and louder. Heat waves above the town, taller and taller. The naked shame of the granite butte growing larger and larger.

Easy Bill was over his horn, his quirt arm was a steel piston he did not have to command.

Jimmy Langman's voice behind him went unheard.

"Wait, Bill. Wait! You're crazy! He's FANNER MARSTEN!"

Fanner Marsten must pay.

Fanner Marsten was waiting, watching, seeing this twin cumulus coming in a land where it never rained. Fanner was waiting with a score-notched gun on each slim hip and a smile on his bitter, twisted face.

Fanner Marsten on the high boardwalk was saying, "Here he comes, boys. That's Easy Bill. His funeral's on me!"

Easy Bill pushed back the canyon walls and thundered down the narrow pass. Jimmy Langman swerved around the turn behind him, quirt falling, young face drawn, blond hair white as lime from lather and alkali.

Something had to stop Easy Bill.

Something, anything . . .

"Wait!" cried Smiling Jimmy, his voice as hoarse and raw as a stamping mill. He swallowed the dust of his words as he cried, "Bill! You're crazy! He's FANNER MARSTEN!"

Something had to stop him this side of death. Something, anything . . .

Ahead, Easy Bill streaked down toward a brace of guardian redcoat stones. He did not see the burro and rider until he had almost run them down. And then it was the gray who did the thinking.

Buster reared and slashed air as he skidded to a smoking stop. Easy Bill's eyes never left the street which had been bared to his ice-chip glare.

Without looking down he yelled in a voice as foreign to him as the wrath.

"Get out of my way!"

Buster reared again, half-mad from the lashing quirt. The burro stayed across the path, chewing spiny cactus with a zinc-lined mouth.

A man came up on the other side of the dun and dusty pack animal. It was Rocky Leonard, bearded and fat and forlorn.

"Easy Bill!" cried Rocky. "I knowed you'd come, you damn fool. He's waiting for you!"

Easy Bill looked down when he heard the voice and stayed his quirt hand. But none of the madness went out of his glance.

"Is he in town?" snapped Easy Bill.

"You didn't think he'd run from the likes of you, didya? He's FANNER MARSTEN, Easy. He's the best in the state. Maybe the best in the West. He's killed forty-one men, counting Mexicans. I ain't goin' to let you be the forty-second."

"Get out of my way!"

"You ain't no gunman, Easy," pleaded Rocky. The fat wrinkles around his eyes were drawn up tight with worry, his beard stuck straight out with determination. "You ain't goin' to get by!"

Easy Bill saw it was Rocky, then.

But his voice didn't let down and his glance did not relent. "You saw him kill Bob?"

7

"I was on the walk above Bob when it happened."

"Where's Bob?"

"We laid him out in the Oasis Saloon on a billiard table."

"Was it an even break?"

"Didn't Jimmy tell you when he took you the news?"

There was neither tone nor flexibility to Easy Bill's sharp voice.

"Was it an even break?"

"Now, Easy. Don't get yourself killed. He's waiting for you. He's bragging, making bets on where he'll hit you. He never misses. He's so fast you can't see his hand move when he draws. You ain't no gunman, Easy. I'll go get your brother and you can take him home."

"WAS IT AN EVEN BREAK?"

Rocky shifted his glance. He felt like crying.

Rocky looked back and the ice-chip eyes pried the truth out of him.

"Bob said any gunman was a skunk at heart and Marsten heard him. . . ."

"Quick!"

"Bob was drunk. He didn't know what he was sayin'. Fanner drew without sayin' a thing and shot Bob three times before we even knowed it was goin' to happen."

"That's all I want to know. GET OUT OF MY WAY!"

The quirt arm came down again with a sharp crack. Smiling Jimmy came to a panting, glad stop on Easy Bill's right.

"Hold him, Rocky!"

"I'm doin' my best," called Rocky on the burro's far side.

Smiling Jimmy made a grab for Easy's arm and got it,

almost pulling Easy off the gray. Easy did not know what he was doing. His quirt came over in a swishing curve and cracked against Smiling Jimmy's jaw.

Jimmy let go. But he did not feel the growing sting of the long, red welt. He tried for another hold.

"You ain't no gunman!" shouted Jimmy. "He'll murder you without trying! Easy. For God's sake, I wouldn't have told you if I'd known. . . ."

"Bob was drunk!" chimed Rocky across the blocking burro. "He said—"

"GET OUT OF MY WAY!" roared Easy Bill.

Jimmy's hold slipped loose. The quirt struck him and then whipped back to come crashing like a rifle shot on the gray's rump.

Buster, mouth raw, out of his head, tried to whirl. The curb tightened and kept him straight. The quirt exploded again.

Buster soared straight out and over, heels clearing the burro by inches. Rocky threw himself back out of danger. The gray hurtled down into the single heat-whipped street of Red Butte.

Fanner Marsten had been waiting. He stepped a pace forward, giving his black slouch hat a rakish tug over his slitted left eye. The other was wide open, watchful.

"Hold your ears, boys," said Fanner without turning to the hastily withdrawing crowd.

The gray streaked up the street, with the color of dust and the speed of light. Easy Bill saw Fanner Marsten. He jerked hard and stood Buster straight up.

The ice-chip eyes were as frozen as Easy Bill's brain. The

hat dropped back, released by the wind, and the chin thong welt was like a bullet crease across his lean jaw.

Buster's four hoofs were on the sandy earth again and Easy Bill came out of the saddle, stiff as a walking poker.

He dropped the reins and stepped toward the boardwalk, looking up at the man in black-and-white who stood there grinning at him. Sun flashed as it ricocheted from the clean gunhawk's .45s.

Easy Bill went up to the walk as though shot from a cannon. He stopped twenty feet from Fanner Marsten.

To Easy Bill everything was clear and chill. He was conscious of nothing but the gun at his side and the man in black-and-white before him.

"You killed Bob Gates this afternoon," said Easy Bill in a toneless, sharp voice.

Fanner Marsten grinned at his forty-second notch-to-be. He was having his fun in the way he liked best.

"Nobody ever told me his brother was good with a gun."

"You didn't give him an even break," said Easy Bill, monotonous and hard as a steel rail.

"You going to do something about it?" replied Fanner with a sweet, innocent smile, as inviting as a worthless woman's smirk.

"I aim to even up the board," said Easy Bill, looking straight ahead and feeling the weight of the gun on his hip without touching it.

"Any time you say, pardner," grinned Fanner Marsten. "I never in my life seen a man so anxious to die. Soon as you move, we draw and blaze away. Fun, huh?"

*Buster's four hoofs were on the sandy earth again and
Easy Bill came out of the saddle, stiff as a walking poker.*

Easy Bill would not have felt a branding iron then. He was an arm, a pair of eyes and a gun. Beyond Fanner he could see the door of the Oasis. Bob was in there, on a billiard table, arms crossed on his riddled chest. . . .

Fanner was grinning more widely, watching Easy Bill's eyes.

"Why did you kill him?" said Easy Bill without moving.

"There was a good reason," said Fanner.

"You wanted me to come in here to finish it off so you could get us both," said Easy Bill.

Everything was clear to him. The boards were a pattern of cracks he had never seen before. The nails in the sidewalk were standing out, each one separate.

The buttons on Fanner's fancy vest were sharp, down to the last carefully threaded hole.

"Are you going to move?" said Fanner, getting a little bored. "It ain't everybody I give an even break."

"Barton hired you. He wants our spread," said Easy Bill without any change in his voice whatever.

Fanner was growing impatient. It was hot in the sun and the flies were buzzing around a black spot near his boots—from which they had picked up Bob Gates. The flies tickled Fanner's face as they rose up and batted against him.

He raised his hand suddenly, angrily, to brush them away.

Easy Bill had not been watching Fanner's eyes. His mind was centered on Bob Gates inside the Oasis.

Fanner's hand moved suddenly, coming up past his right gun butt. Easy Bill saw it and acted, knowing he was about to die. But he did not care about that. He had had to come.

Easy Bill's fingers went down, flawless and swift. No gunman, but he could draw. Fanner's .45s would be out and smoking before his own ever left leather.

Fanner saw the move the instant Easy Bill touched his gun.

Fanner was off balance. He brought his right hand down, conscious only of the fact that it had betrayed him. He was not cool in that instant.

Fanner's hand smacked against the walnut butt. Steel flashed in the blinding sunlight as the .45 came up.

Easy Bill had the start.

Easy Bill's hand was still going down. He tipped the butt back, finger in the guard, on the trigger. He raised the weapon, holster and all, twisting sideways to do it.

Fanner fired in haste.

Easy Bill fired through the bottom of his leather. The kick jabbed the .45 free into Easy Bill's hand.

Fanner was starting to turn around. He whipped back, left hand down for its gun. Left gun out before the right-hand .45 had reached the boards.

Easy Bill fired again.

Twice. Three times. Four times.

The .45 in Easy Bill's hand had jumped up level with his jaw.

Fanner was farther away. He seemed to have stumbled over something.

Five times. Six times.

The hammer clicked on the first. The cylinder had turned all the way around.

So had Fanner Marsten. His boots were working back and

forth, soles toward Easy Bill. Marsten was on his face. His right gun was all alone and his left boot was pointing at it. His left gun was frozen solid in his clutching grasp. They would bury him with it still in his hand.

Easy Bill just stood there.

The world was beginning to whirl and grow dim. He was starting to shake.

Then Smiling Jimmy Langman was beside him, gently pulling him back and away. Rocky was on the other side, looking fixedly at Fanner Marsten's boots now that they were still.

The whole town was held in a silence as thick as the ooze which ran out from under Fanner's chest.

The flies had left the dried, black spot and settled down in a buzzing cloud over the fresh, bright scarlet pool which grew bigger and bigger for them.

Smiling Jimmy got Easy Bill turned around and headed down the walk.

Rocky jerked his thumb at a sagging hotel sign over their heads. Jimmy guided Easy in through the broken-paned door.

A crowd spread back like an unfolding hand of cards.

Jimmy and Rocky kept looking straight ahead. They guided Easy Bill up a flight of creaking, rickety stairs, into a dim and murky hall, through a door.

The broken-backed bed registered on Easy Bill's brain. He turned a little and sat down upon it, staring at the floor.

He felt sick at his stomach. His hands were shaking as he tried to steady his face. The room was spinning faster and faster and Rocky and Jimmy were all mixed up with the crazy windows and splintery chairs and a cracked white washbowl.

Easy Bill tried to focus on the washbowl.

God, but he felt sick!

Chapter Two

GEORGE BARTON'S ranch house and George Barton were both strange to the Silverado country, though both had been there many years.

George Barton was a man of great wealth. At least he often said he was, and men, looking at the deep leather chairs of his house, at the thickness of his rugs, at the beauty of his vests, believed him.

George Barton was a big man. He owned a big ranch. He did everything in a big way. He thought in terms of monopolies, judged men in terms of power and cash (which are the same), and generally made his presence in the Silverado country a most weighty and dictatorial thing.

It was not enough that he owned *El Rancho Grandisimo*. He had to own *Las Piñas* as well.

Why he wanted this power and money no man knew. He had neither wife nor son to carry on in case . . .

Well, there were many men who wanted to murder George Barton.

Three months to the day after the shooting of Fanner Marsten, a strange rider arrived at the Barton ranch. He was dusty and dry and had the appearance of being barrel tanned and his skin nailed back on his bones.

He was six feet four inches tall and weighed less than a

hundred and thirty pounds and he was so loose and rusty you expected his joints to squeak like hinges when he walked.

He entered the Barton house without knocking and without removing his stained wide hat. He looked around the drawing room and listened with his head cocked on one side and his eyes alert. He stepped back to the screen door and looked out at the sizzling day, minutely examining the road over which his dust still hung in the motionless air.

No one had followed him.

No one was behind the door.

No one was visible anywhere with a gun in his hand.

The dry stranger lifted his quirt and brought it down hard on the smooth, shining surface of the library table. It left a round pattern of dust there, cut in two by the dark line of the quirt itself.

The sound brought a round-faced, tiptoeing Chinese out of the kitchen.

"Who you?"

"I'm Spider Harrigan. Where's old man Barton?"

The name frightened the Chinese and he wrung his hands hurriedly upon his white apron.

He chop-chopped with small fast steps toward the rear of the house. As the pit-pat died away, the dusty stranger looked with some suspicion at a case of books against the far wall. Then he saw a rifle hanging to a fine head of horns and his colorless eyes brightened up.

He was stepping forward to take down the gun when the Chinese came back.

"Mr. Barton wait. You come along quick."

The dusty stranger brushed past the little yellow man, going through a space which would not have passed a cat for width.

He strode with jingling spurs toward the far-off door, very alert and very loose, hands dusting the gun on each hip as he walked.

He glimpsed a shadow behind a door and dodged like a shying colt, right hand going down and coming up so swiftly that only the dust its passage left in the air marked the route he had traveled for his gun. He looked closer at the door, swung it back and forth a couple times and then dropped the Colt into its holster. He went on down the hall to the far door and thrust it back.

George Barton was sitting in an easy chair, heels on his rolltop desk, smoking a fat cigar. His brows traveled up and came down again as he saw his caller. He shoved the cigar in his face, worked it around and then hooked his thumbs into his vest. He looked at Spider Harrigan for some time and then brought his heels down out of sight. He leaned forward and unhooked his thumbs. He took the cigar out of his swollen mouth and gave Spider Harrigan the full blast of a pair of light gray orbs.

"You'll do," said George Barton in his cigar-husky voice, which always gave him the look and sound of whispering.

He put the smoke in his mouth, hooked his thumbs in his vest, put his heels on his desk and leaned back in his easy chair.

Spider Harrigan came in a little further and glanced behind

all the doors. Then he saw a chair and flopped up in front of it and bent in the middle and suddenly sat down, looking like a broken stick.

Spider Harrigan spun his quirt around a couple times. It seemed that George Barton had forgotten he was there.

"Maybe I'll do and maybe I won't," said Harrigan, sounding like a rattler's tail buzzing.

George Barton put his heels on the floor again and took the cigar out of his mouth.

"I said you'll do and *you'll do.* How much money do you want?"

"Five a day and ammunition."

George Barton was amused. He began to laugh, his stomach working up and down with never a sound coming out of his throat but the whistle of rough air. In a short while he quieted down again and put the cigar back in his face. He looked at Spider and began to laugh a second time.

Spider came to his feet with a creak and a jingle.

"What's so funny?" he buzzed.

"You," whispered Barton, stifled with mirth, and went back into his paroxysms of silent laughter.

Spider had a horny palm on the butt of each Colt. He studied Barton with his narrow, colorless eyes and finally decided it was all right.

He sat down.

"Go ahead and laugh. When you've finished, we can talk."

Barton came around to face him again.

"Five dollars a day and ammunition!" chuckled Barton. He was on the verge of going off into mirth again but he

20

controlled himself. "You don't even know what I want you to do."

"That ain't my fault. If you'd stop that damned haw-haw-haw and get down to business . . ."

"Shut up. Don't you know who you're talking to?"

Spider sat like a broken stick and said nothing.

"I'm George Barton, the biggest man in Silverado. I own so much land I've lost count of it. I own so many cattle I can't get a crew big enough to brand them. Now do you get my point?"

"I heard about you but I ain't got the point."

"There's ten thousand acres up in the hills north of here. Streams and trees. I've tried to buy it a dozen times but Gates won't sell. *I want Las Piñas* and there's no law but Judge Colt in Silverado. I need those streams, that forest grazing land."

Spider, midway of Barton's speech, had begun to sit up and look jumpy. "Did you say Gates? Easy Bill Gates?"

"Sure I said *Gates.* What about it?"

Spider got up restlessly and went to the window. He peered out toward the corrals and craned his neck so he could see down the road where his own dust had now settled. He took his hand off his gun and came back.

He slapped the desk with his quirt. "No sale."

"You haven't heard my price. Sit down!"

"There ain't any price where that guy is concerned. I heard it at Abilene two months ago. He killed Fanner Marsten on an even break and Fanner was first to his irons. Fanner Marsten was the fastest man but one in this country."

"Who's the one?"

21

"Greaser Rawkins. He was faster than Fanner Marsten. Still is." Spider leaned tensely across the table. "You think I'm out of my mind? You think I'm such a goddamn fool I'd swap smoke with Easy Bill Gates?"

Barton began to laugh again, soundlessly, the air rushing in and out below his scraggly gray mustache. He finally stopped and looked up at Spider.

"Marsten was the only man Gates ever killed."

Spider drew back. "Yeah, but Marsten killed forty-one, counting Mexicans. Not me, Barton."

Barton was very amused. He chewed his cigar all around his mouth and then leaned forward.

"One thousand dollars cash if you *bushwhack* Gates."

Spider looked up. He was interested now. "You mean get him with a Sharps on the trail? Without him knowing anything about it?"

"That's the general idea."

"Get him without his having a chance to go for his gun?"

"That's it."

"Knock him kicking with a slug at long range without him ever hearing the sound of the shot?"

"Right."

Spider grinned, breaking the caked alkali on his face.

"Okay, Barton. What's he look like, where's he live, and how much money do I get down?"

Barton began to tell him but Spider could only rock on his heels and grin and mutter to himself. "Wait 'til it gets around that *I* downed the man who killed Fanner Marsten! Wait until . . ."

Chapter Three

EASY BILL GATES was himself again. He sat with his high heels on the rail and leaned his chair back into the cool of the shadowy veranda.

Rocky Leonard was sitting on his lowest step, whittling thoughtfully and cluttering up the sandy front yard with splinters which blew around in the wind that had come up as the sun started down.

"You're in for trouble, Easy Bill," said Rocky.

"Aw," drawled Easy, sucking on his pipe, "nobody wants to get even with me. Fanner didn't have any friends and Barton knows better than to try anything else. I think I come off riding straight up and fanning my bronc."

"Sure. Sure you did, Bill. I never did see no guy that was so eager to meet his Maker as you was that day. But you ain't no gunman, and don't start thinkin' you are."

"Me?" laughed Easy Bill, taking a comfortable drag. "Me a gunman?" He laughed again, sighting down his long legs between his boot toes at the blazing sunset beyond. "I couldn't hit you from where I'm sitting, Rocky. Not with a scatter-gun."

"I know it," said Rocky. "That's what got me worried."

A trotting horse around the corner of the house made them stop and look in that direction. It was Jimmy Langman.

The youth swung down and left his reins dragging,

mounting the porch rail as though it was a bucking horse. He grinned at Rocky and then turned to Easy Bill, about to say something.

Easy Bill looked curiously at Smiling Jimmy's cheek as though seeing it for the first time.

"Where'd you get that welt, Jimmy?"

"What?"

"That long bruise on the side of your face. I saw it a couple weeks ago but never really noticed it 'til now. Looks like somebody hit you with a quirt."

"Well . . ." Jimmy looking uneasily at Rocky down below him. "Yeah. Sure. Somebody hit me with a quirt."

Easy Bill let his curiosity rest. He was too comfortable sitting there on his veranda looking out at the sunset through the pines.

Jimmy faced him again. "I'm worried, Bill."

"That's strange. Don't recall you being worried before."

Jimmy nodded. "But this is enough to worry anybody."

Rocky stopped whittling and looked up like a man who has been expecting bad news for a long time. He scratched his beard wearily and waited.

"Spider Harrigan was seen over by Cougar Canyon today. Loftus was telling me. He looked like he come far and fast, Bill."

"Well?" said Easy Bill, barely interested.

"You know Spider Harrigan's reputation," said Jimmy.

"Sure. Killer. What's he doing in this country?"

"That's what I want to know," said Jimmy. "He's lightning

hybrid with a rattlesnake. I . . . I think he came down here to nail you, Bill."

"Me?" said Easy Bill, setting back all four legs of his chair. Then he shrugged and grinned and sucked at his pipe. "You're crazy, Jimmy. Been eatin' locoweed." He laughed about it to himself.

Jimmy looked for a long time at Easy Bill's smooth, unworried face. It was hard to imagine Bill getting mad. Hard to imagine Bill standing up and facing Fanner Marsten. Rage had done that, nothing more. Never again in his life would Bill be that sore about anything.

"There's also a rumor," said Jimmy, "that Greaser Rawkins is heading this way. He was Fanner Marsten's best friend."

"Nobody is going to try anything," said Easy Bill. "Calm down. Ain't that a beautiful sunset?"

Rocky got up and walked down the path. He turned and came back and went up the steps and leaned himself against the pillar near Jimmy's boots.

"Bill," said Rocky. "You're a lot bigger fool than even I thought you was. You always was the most easygoin', don't-give-a-damn cuss in these parts. I used to think you was smart. 'Now take Bill,' I'd say to myself, 'there is one gent that won't never git nobody riled up. Most likely he'll die with his boots off of old age.'

"And now look what you've done," said Rocky, growing more vehement. "You kill the worst killer these parts has ever known. You put yourself on a glory stand and asks all the gents from the Mississip to Denver to come around and try

25

their luck at you. You got a *reputation* because you drawed faster than Marsten.

"I've heerd a lot of things about you in the last three months. I've heerd fellers swapping the damnedest lies about how good you was with a gun. You're a marked man and you take my word for it, you better get out and practice the draw plenty."

Smiling Jimmy looked grave. "Greaser Rawkins seems to feel pretty cut up about you being a better gunman than he is."

"Forget it," ordered Easy Bill, drawing contentedly upon his pipe.

He was lulled by the splendor of the sunset and the peace of a departing day. Fanner Marsten seemed very far away, just then.

Easy Bill had, for the past ten minutes, been watching a sparkle he had caught on a nearby knoll. Some ragged rocks up there evidently had some crystal quartz in them. The sun, going down, had struck fire. At first he had had the idea that it might be a gun barrel, but he had banished this as silly.

The wind was sighing in the pines and the day was still. Twilight would be there in a few minutes and the night which followed would be restful and cool.

Smiling Jimmy and Rocky were looking at each other with some little disgust. Rocky sat down on the upper step and started whittling again, faster now, viciously.

Jimmy swung his boots and looked at the comfortable length of Easy Bill. No man had ever had a more pleasant face, a more ready smile. Bob Gates had been very like him but Bob Gates had always drunk too much.

"Greaser Rawkins," said Jimmy, "was Fanner Marsten's best friend. He's dynamite. He'd rather shoot a man in the back but he's got guts enough to stand up for an even break and speed enough to get out of it. He was better than Fanner, Bill. A hell of a lot better than Fanner Marsten ever was. You played right into Barton's hands that time."

"Drop it," said Easy Bill, indolently watching the sparkle of metal on the knoll—which looked so much like crystal quartz. "Barton won't bother us."

"No?" spat Rocky. "Sometimes, Bill, I don't think you even got good sense. Whether you like it or not you killed yourself a reputation and that was just what Barton wanted."

"Oh, I don't know," said Easy Bill.

"*I* know," said Jimmy. "Hasn't he tried to buy *Las Piñas*? He needs our streams and woodland when the weather gets hot."

"If he'd offer a decent price . . ." said Easy Bill.

"It's cheaper," said Jimmy, "to have you killed now that Bob has gone."

"Barton wouldn't do that," said Easy Bill. "I thought he sicced Fanner on to us, but maybe I was wrong. No use jumping at conclusions."

"You make me sick," said Rocky, throwing down his stick and pocketing his knife.

Jimmy, as the *Las Piñas* foreman, had work to do that night. He slid down off the rail and followed Rocky out along the path.

Easy Bill got up and leaned against the porch pillar, a

27

beautiful target as the dying rays of the sun hit him full. He started to hook a finger in his cartridge belt.

Abruptly two shells exploded hot against his hand. A mighty hammer had struck him in the middle, turning his belt, breaking the thongs, throwing Easy Bill violently backward into the darkness of the porch. A delayed report came from afar.

He lay flat on his face, gasping, trying to get his breath. His shirt was burning and he could feel hot blood running down his thigh.

He rolled over on his side and slapped the fire out. He put his hand under his belt to see how badly he was hit.

Jimmy and Rocky had whirled as though to start back. They changed their minds and dived into the cover of a grove of pines.

A Winchester had leaped magically from its boot into Jimmy's hands.

He leveled it now, toward a puff of white smoke on the knoll. The range was too far but Jimmy let drive.

He emptied his magazine and reloaded from his chaps pocket and again raised his rifle.

Rocky pushed the barrel down. "Don't waste it. That guy has gone this long time, son."

They ran back to the porch and found Easy Bill taking off his shirt, still seated on the 'dobe floor.

"Splinters," said Easy Bill, looking down. "The half-baked idiot shot at the flash of the cartridges in my belt!"

"And he hit 'em too," said Rocky, going inside to get the cook and bandages.

Jimmy looked at Easy Bill, almost laughing. "So you didn't believe it, huh? So you didn't believe that Spider came up here to kill you, huh? You're a killer now, old son. You can't be trusted on an even break. It's got to be a bushwhack job."

"Does Spider know this country?" said Easy Bill.

"No. I don't think so."

"Then he'll take to the flats. I'm going to get to Barton before he does."

Rocky returned and heard the last words. "You damn fool! You ain't mad even now. You never did get mad when somebody did something to *you*. You stay here and let Barton be. He's got a ranch swarmin' with punchers and bristling with artillery."

"Get my gray," said Easy Bill.

He seemed to think it was funny, somehow. Jimmy and Rocky sighed in unison and went to do his bidding.

Chapter Four

G EORGE BARTON was waiting.
He was sitting behind his desk with his heels up on a drawn-out leaf, watching the gyrations of a moth above his oil lamp. The moth persisted in dipping down at the chimney top, soaring up and away as it was caught in the rising current of heated air.

But each time the moth returned to dive again.

George Barton was very absorbed. Since darkness had fallen he had been watching that moth flutter and bank and soar around the chimney.

The silvery gray wings were tireless. The determination of the thing was amazing. George Barton was spellbound.

Far off he heard the clatter of approaching hoofs and looked up just as though a man of his high caliber could see through thick 'dobe and pierce the velvet night.

It could not be one of his boys. They were mostly at their line camps or in the faraway bunkhouses. It must therefore be Spider Harrigan returning with excellent news.

George Barton grinned with satisfaction. He reached up and swiped his hand through the air before the moth and caught the silvery gray wings in his heavy grasp. It beat against the soft flesh, trying valiantly to escape.

George Barton carefully lifted the moth up and gave a downward toss. The silvery gray wings charred when they hit the flame inside the chimney.

The horse had stopped outside. Leather creaked. A heavy boot sounded on the top step and then spurs jingle bobbed merrily as the rider crossed to the door.

There was only one light in the house and the rider would, of course, head for that light.

The horse moved off slowly, looking for grass, pausing and going on until George knew it was behind the ranch house.

A door slammed and from the vigor of it, Barton guessed at good news. The jingle bobs came clinking down the hall and the study door swung in.

Barton was just about to say, "Hello, Spider," when he happened to look up.

His mouth dropped open and he was hurled by surprise back into his swivel chair.

"Hello, Barton," said Easy Bill Gates.

Barton's first thought was toward his center drawer where he kept a chubby little Derringer. He knew better than to make a move. He sat with his hands pitifully away from anything suspicious.

Easy Bill drew up a chair and sat down. He stuffed some fresh tobacco into his pipe, shoved his wide hat to the back of his blond head and struck a match to light up.

"Spider Harrigan called," said Easy Bill with a grin.

"You killed him?" gasped Barton.

"No such luck. He was too jittery to show himself. What's the idea, Barton?"

32

"Idea? Why, my dear fellow," said Barton, getting back his poise, "if you think I had anything to do with—"

"Don't lie to me, Barton," said Easy Bill, grinning and settling back in his chair. "You hired my brother killed and now you're trying to hire me dead. It's not the thing to do, Barton."

Barton felt greatly wronged, though he was guilty. He felt very virtuous and feudal.

"What's the idea coming to my house?" growled Barton in sudden heat. Now that he knew Easy Bill had come to talk and not kill, Barton's courage flooded back.

"I wanted to talk this over with you," said Easy Bill. "You own most of Silverado and you want *Las Piñas*. I can't sell at the price you offered me."

"I offered you fair money!" snapped Barton. "You can't come here and try to intimidate—"

"If you're intimidated," drawled Easy Bill, "I shore am some flattered, Barton."

George Barton remembered then that he was *the* lord of Silverado. "You came to take me up on my offer?"

"I don't want trouble, Barton. If you want *Las Piñas,* pay me for what it's worth and I'll drift west. I've wanted to go for some time."

"I've offered you all I ever will, Gates!"

"You'd have to double it. I'm a peaceful man, Barton. I don't want any range war bubbling up around here. I don't want Jimmy Langman dead. Fanner Marsten killed Bob. I evened it up and I'm satisfied. But if you want *Las Piñas,* pay for it like a man and don't hire me killed like a skunk."

33

Perhaps the truth of the statement hurt George Barton's sensitive nature. Perhaps it was because George Barton had detected the far-off rattle of approaching hoofs and knew that Spider was on his way. No man had ever beaten Spider to the draw.

Barton came up out of his seat and poked his fat face at Easy Bill.

"All right!" roared Barton. "You asked for it! You either sell at my price or I'll see you buried!"

"You mean that?" said Easy Bill. "Why, that sounds mighty like blackmail or something of the sort, Barton."

"Call it what you like, you fool. Take it or leave it. If Spider Harrigan can't do the job, Greaser Rawkins will. Now talk and talk fast. Do you sell at my price or do you get buried for yours?"

Easy Bill sighed. "An' I thought I could talk this over quiet-like." He heaved another sigh and stuck his pipe in his mouth.

The sound of hoofs had ceased with Easy Bill's hearing them. He forgot the moon was coming up and that his horse might be visible outside. He had no definite plan because he relied too much on men and had never been able to quite believe what he really knew about Barton.

A board creaked on the porch and a hinge groaned. Easy Bill heard it. He stood up with a warning glance at Barton and turned to face the door.

There was a vase on the bookcase beside him, slightly in advance of his eyes. Back of the vase was a mirror and Barton knew Easy Bill was watching him in that.

A board creaked in the hall.

Spider Harrigan was cautious by nature—which was why he had lived this long. He had not seen a horse but he was taking no chances and never did.

He laid his hand on the knob of the door and slowly pushed inward.

He saw Barton standing like a lump of dough beside his desk.

The light from the lamp was in Spider's eyes when he turned slightly and caught a glimpse of Easy Bill.

Easy Bill had not drawn his gun. He was standing there wondering what was going to happen next, believing implicitly that Spider would try nothing, having once failed.

Spider Harrigan knew what he was looking at. He was still a little blind but there was no mistaking the slouch of the man before him. Spider thought there was a gun in Bill's hand, it had happened so fast. But the glint was only glass in the bookcase.

The terrified lurch of Spider's body against the door immediately preceded his draw.

He had never been beaten and he knew it.

Spider grabbed walnut in a swooping dive.

His right gun came up before Easy Bill had started to draw. Flame ribboned away from Spider's side.

The vase before Easy Bill and the mirror behind it crashed in countless silver splinters.

Easy Bill dropped into a crouch as his gun came free. Spider fired again.

Pain was jagged through Bill's left shoulder.

Easy Bill drew his bead and fired.

A round hole appeared in Spider's dusty shirt. His left gun sent a slug straight down into the floor. He sagged against the door. It gave way slowly, letting him inch down toward the rug.

Abruptly, Spider bent like a broken match and crashed with a jingle of spurs to the floor.

Barton stood staring at the long, bent body.

Easy Bill coughed from the acrid fumes of black powder. He dropped his Colt into its holster and pushed it solidly down.

He walked forward, almost tripped over Spider. He felt for the doorway and went through. He ran his hand along the side of the wall toward the outer entrance.

Barton had not dared to move. He did not even dare to breathe. He stood there and looked at the gunman's corpse and heard Easy Bill's faltering boots going away, heard Easy Bill whistle for Buster.

Easy Bill crawled laboriously into the saddle and Buster moved away at a walk. Men were running up from the bunkhouses but they did not stop him or shoot.

A rolling, running thunder of hoofs was coming up the road. It was Jimmy, unable to longer obey his orders to stay home.

"You all right, Bill?" said Smiling Jimmy, very concerned.

"I'm all right," said Easy Bill.

"You're hit!"

"Hit, Jimmy? Am I?"

"Sure! There's blood on your shoulder!" Jimmy reined

closer. "And there's a million cuts around your eyes. What happened?"

"I don't know, Jimmy. I guess he's dead."

"You *guess* he's dead?"

"Yes, Jimmy."

Smiling Jimmy leaned forward in sudden fear. He passed his hand before Easy Bill's eyes and Easy Bill did not blink.

"My God," whispered Jimmy. "He's *blind*!"

Chapter Five

DOC SPRIGGS, originally a barber by trade, was very conversational. Small and bearded and red of eye, he was peculiarly distinguished by the tweed suit he wore in a land where leather and flannel were the only goods known.

He fussed over Easy Bill in his easy chair upon the veranda and discoursed to the ranch hands at large—most of which were gathered along the rail hopelessly looking toward Easy Bill.

"Greaser Rawkins hit town today," said Doc Spriggs, working an eye bandage clumsily into place on Easy Bill's head. "First piece of news that's happened in a month—ever since you shot up Spider Harrigan, in fact."

The punchers had stiffened along the rail. Rocky and Smiling Jimmy were looking at each other.

Doc Spriggs felt nothing of the sudden electric shock, principally because it is hard for a man to feel anything when he has drunk a quart for breakfast.

Doc Spriggs forgot what he was doing for the moment and stood up importantly. "*I* patched Greaser Rawkins together one time when a Mex walked around him with a knife. That was in Dodge City. I even seen the fight."

This was quite a bit of glory for one man. It could be told by the way he said it.

"The Mex," said Spriggs, "sneaked up on the Greaser when he was asleep because the Greaser had shot the Mex's boss in a fair fight the day before. The Mex sinks about six inches of steel into the Greaser before Rawkins knew what was happening to him.

"But the Greaser was game. He reached out and got his gun and he did it so fast that before the Mex could move, there were six bullets in him. The Greaser practically blew out his whole backside.

"And then the Greaser gets up and takes the knife out of himself and bends over the Mex and very carefully cuts the dead man's head off. He takes it outside and hangs it on his rack with its own hair. And it wasn't until then that he sent for me to mend a wound that would of killed ten ordinary men."

Warningly, Rocky said, "How's Easy Bill's eyes?"

Doc Spriggs got back on his job again. He put two cotton pads soaked in boric acid under the bandage and then stood back to look judicially at his patient.

"Well," said Doc Spriggs, "I tell you. He's got about a fifty-fifty chance."

"Rats," said Easy Bill unexpectedly. "I could see daylight through the gauze when you had the bandage off."

"Still," said Doc Spriggs, "I took six slivers of glass out of the pupils and they ain't had much time to heal. Maybe you will and maybe you won't, but it's a cinch your eyesight ain't never going to be a hell of a lot of good to you anymore."

This cheering news reminded the doc of another story. "I

40

recall once this here Greaser Rawkins got a bullet in him at long range. Right in his thigh. This was up in the Rio Nardas country—or was it near San Antone. No, it was Rio Nardas. Anyhow, this Greaser Rawkins was riding along and he gets this bullet in him. He drops off his horse just as nice as you please and lays there like he was dead.

"Pretty soon a young puncher—the Greaser had killed one of his friends in an even break except that the friend's gun wasn't loaded and the Greaser knowed it—pretty soon this young puncher come down to look over his handiwork. And he stands right there with a Sharps in his hands looking down at Greaser Rawkins not two feet away.

"And before the puncher could move that gun barrel around and pull the trigger, the Greaser had drawed and sent three shots into him just like that. The Greaser hung him by his heels from a cactus and went on into town to get patched up."

The punchers were all waiting for Spriggs to go so that they could damn his soul to eternity. But they were polite so far.

"There's your buckboard and here's ten bucks," said Smiling Jimmy with a very disgusted expression.

"Oh, I got lots of time," said Doc Spriggs. "I remember when this here Greaser Rawkins—"

"There's your buckboard," said Smiling Jimmy, taking the doc by the arm and signing Rocky to bring the tools.

Doc Spriggs found himself sitting in his buckboard. Rocky lifted the black bag up beside him and glanced back toward the house.

"Doc," said Rocky in a chilling voice which would have

41

made an Apache faint, "if you so much as breathe one word about Easy Bill's eyes, I'll cut out your heart with a dull knife."

"Oh, I won't. I won't. But he's so fast on the draw . . ."

"On your way," said Smiling Jimmy, hand resting lightly on the butt of his gun.

Doc Spriggs picked up his reins and made a clucking sound. The buckboard began to roll down the hill toward the bare valley visible through the pines.

Doc Spriggs was not thinking at all. He was merely riding and driving.

He took—very automatically—a bottle from under the seat blanket and upended it against his mouth. He put the cork and bottle back and looked up to see that he had come farther than he had thought.

He went even further before anything jolted itself into his foggy consciousness.

George Barton on a big black stallion was barring the road between two canyon walls. He was just on the edge of *Las Piñas*.

Doc Spriggs drew up with a salute.

Barton made no introduction. "You just came from Easy Bill Gates."

"Sure. Say, ain't that boy hell on wheels with a gun, though? Fanner Marsten and then Spider Harrigan. Wouldn't be surprised if Greaser Rawkins didn't come down here just to put a very fancy notch on his gun. But Easy Bill . . ."

Barton's cigar-husky voice sawed its way into the doc's mind. "How is Easy Bill getting along?"

"He's fine."

"Didn't he get hit in the mess with Spider?"

"Sure. In the left shoulder. But hell, Barton, that healed up three days ago complete."

"Then what were you doing up there?"

"It was his eyes."

"Eyes?"

Doc Spriggs nodded and dug the bottle out of the blanket. "Drink? No? Well, it's mighty dry today. I hear . . ."

Barton put both hands on his silvered horn and looked carefully at Doc Spriggs. "You said something about his eyes."

"I'm not supposed to tell," said Doc Spriggs. "But you're a big man around here, Barton."

"Sure I am. What about Easy Bill's eyes?"

"Spider hit a vase alongside of his head and filled the pupils full of glass splinters. It ain't likely he'll ever be able to see again worth a nickel."

"Is that so," said Barton. He dug into his belt and pulled out five double eagles which he tossed heavily into the buckboard one by one.

"Make sure you don't tell anyone else, Spriggs."

The doc was busy gathering up the double eagles. He looked knowingly at Barton.

"No. Not a soul. I ain't so drunk as I look sometimes, Barton."

But Barton was already riding fast down the canyon in the direction of Red Butte.

Chapter Six

GREASER RAWKINS lay on the hot side of a ridge. The sun was showering molten arrows into his back and pounding heat waves out of the ground and into his face. His Sharps was hot enough to char his hands.

But Greaser Rawkins lay there quite content, quite like a horny Gila monster with its prey in sight.

The face beneath the battered hat was so lined with scars and plowed with bullets that it resembled more of a contour map of battles than a human visage. The hand on the trigger had such a calloused index finger that it was a wonder it had any feeling in it at all.

Short and warped and evil, Greaser Rawkins broiled himself on the lava. He was too thin to have any suet in him, too light to leave any impression in the dust on which he lay.

The scorching wind which curled and charred the grass on its way up from the simmering valley had carried to him the sound of a horse's hoofs and the clink of a spur.

Three hundred yards below and ahead of him a narrow defile led its way through the ridge, marking the boundary of *Las Piñas*. It was from there that the sounds had come.

He had ears, did the Greaser, and he had eyes. He had thirst and lust. These and these only were his total emotions.

He carefully raised the sights on his Sharps and looked

down them experimentally. A certain heaviness caused by
the presence of double eagles in his pocket was comfortable
under him.

They'd buy lots of whiskey.

The Greaser felt the need of that whiskey right now. For
two weeks he had been walking straight up but completely
unconscious. People that morning had told him Barton wanted
to see him.

Well, to hell with Barton.

Barton was good for another stack of yellow coins. The
Greaser knew that he had better do this job while he thought
about it so that he could later collect.

The man who had killed Fanner Marsten, eh? The guy
who had faced Spider Harrigan, huh?

Sharps at long range cured people of yammering for an
even break.

Greaser Rawkins looked into his chamber and saw the
long brass shell shining there. He grinned with satisfaction.
Again he had heard the roll of a rock disturbed by a horse's hoof.

Easy Bill Gates, in spite of Rocky's warnings and Smiling
Jimmy's loud protests, was taking a circle around *Las Piñas*. It
felt good to ride again after two months on his back looking
at blackness.

Buster had gotten fat and sleek during that time and all day
he had been skittish and full of ginger. It was for this reason
that Easy Bill rode in advance of Smiling Jimmy Langman.

Easy Bill pulled up in the shady side of the defile and

looked out through the hot day at the parching plains which lay beyond. Things were somewhat blurry to him but he could make out a bunched herd of cattle trying to find shade under a stand of bleak Joshua trees.

With some care, Easy Bill steadied his gaze upon them and made out at last that they were very poor specimens of the bovine race.

Smiling Jimmy came up and pulled in beside his friend and boss.

"Are those Barton's?" said Easy Bill, jerking his head toward the herd.

Smiling Jimmy eased it a bit. "Hard to read the brand from here," he lied. "Yes, they're Barton's. They look pretty thin."

"I thought so," said Easy Bill. "Not much more than mud in the water holes down here. Seems like a shame to have all that water going to waste up at *Las Piñas*."

He turned in his saddle and looked back and up toward the hills where his ranch lay.

"Not much grass down here either," said Easy Bill, thinking about his own verdant woodlands.

"You starting to feel sorry for that weasel Barton?"

"No," said Easy Bill. "For his cows."

A rattlesnake crawled from under a cactus, saw the horses and slithered back, buzzing and angry.

Easy Bill heard the buzz and looked carefully at the snake—which was very plain to Jimmy Langman. Easy Bill took some little time locating it.

At last he said triumphantly, "THERE he is!"

47

"I didn't see him myself until just now," lied Smiling Jimmy with a grin.

Easy Bill jolted the .45 out of his holster and juggled it in his palm. He had not fired a shot since that night at Barton's. He was half afraid to try, glancing sideways at Jimmy.

Jimmy whistled elaborately and studied the sides of the defile.

Easy Bill looked back and searched again for the rattler. Then he brought the Colt up to the level of his shirt pocket and looked closely at the rattler. He could see the head—a dark dot in the shadows under the cactus. He had never sighted a Colt in his life but he needed the clarity of vision to line up his target.

He cocked the .45 and looked again at Jimmy. But Jimmy had gotten down to tighten his cinch from the other side.

Easy Bill pulled the trigger.

Through the streak of white smoke, sand leaped up. The rattler was still there.

Easy Bill fired again.

The buzzing continued.

Easy Bill dropped a third shot under the cactus and the buzzing stopped.

"You got him," said Jimmy, looking up in some relief.

"On the third shot," said Easy Bill.

"Your eyes need some rest," said Smiling Jimmy. "This sun is a pretty bad dose for them. Let's be getting back."

They turned their horses and rode up the defile back toward the hills and *Las Piñas.*

Greaser Rawkins was sliding backwards down the slope, dots of sweat on his scarred brow. He raised himself once or twice to make certain he was not being followed.

Finally he reached the ravine and his horse. He mounted hurriedly, still gripping the Sharps.

"Jesus!" said Greaser Rawkins. "Jesus!"

He neck-reined his mustang and dug spur.

As he went swiftly away he looked back.

"He was shootin' at me," moaned Greaser Rawkins. "At *me*! And I never seen so much as a glint below. I see right now this has got to be fast and in the back.

"But how the hell am I going to get him into Red Butte?"

Chapter Seven

THREE days later, Rocky Leonard led his string of pack burros into the corral at *Las Piñas* and closed the gate on them without starting to unpack.

He started toward the line of 'dobes some distance from the ranch house, walking so hard he sent the dust as high as his knees. He was breathing like a mad bull. His black whiskers stood out straight and a man could have lit a cigarette on one of his eyes.

Growling and puffing, he swerved to the left toward the small dun-colored hut which was Smiling Jimmy's quarters as foreman. He went straight in, practically knocking down the door.

He stood there in the center of a red Navajo rug breathing brimstone and spitting flame.

Smiling Jimmy came up off his bunk and put his weekly paper aside. He smiled a welcome and then saw that something was drastically wrong.

"Why, Rocky, what's the matter?"

Rocky stuck out his lower jaw and his teeth flashed in his beard. With some effort he controlled himself enough to talk.

"I was inta Red Butte for supplies."

"Sure. I sent you, didn't I?"

"Yeah. I wisht ta Christ you hadn't!"

Smiling Jimmy's grin faded. "Did the Greaser . . . ?"

"Naw. He wasn't payin' any attention to me. He didn't know who I was. He was standing up at the bar in the Coyote settin' up the drinks and braggin' about how he was goin' to down Easy Bill."

"Sure. Sure. But calm down, Rocky. Take it easy."

"He was callin' Easy Bill every rotten name he could think of—and Greaser Rawkins can think of plenty. He said Easy Bill was a killer and not even a good killer. He said he was goin' to get even—"

"Sure. We all know about the Greaser and Fanner Marsten. Calm down, Rocky. I knew that that was goin' on."

"Yeah?" spat Rocky. "Yeah? You didn't, did you? Well, you don't know the rest of it. Greaser Rawkins was braggin' that Easy Bill was afraid of him."

"He is," said Smiling Jimmy. "Easy Bill's no gunman and now that his eyes—"

"He said he had sent word out here three times for Easy Bill to come in and face him and Easy Bill hadn't arrived. He said Easy Bill shot Spider in the back and tricked Marsten. He said Easy Bill was scared of him, Greaser Rawkins. He said Easy Bill was *yellah*!"

Jimmy stood up and looked at Rocky for a long time. Then he slowly turned to the wooden peg which held his belt and gun. He took down the leather and began to buckle it on. A queer light danced in his usually mild eyes.

Rocky suddenly saw his error.

"Wait! Wait, Jimmy. Hell, I didn't mean . . ."

"Yeah. I know what you meant. Easy Bill isn't yellow but there's only one way to shut the Greaser's mouth."

Jimmy was tying the thongs around his right leg. His hands were shaking a little.

"Wait, Jimmy!" pleaded Rocky. "Don't do this. You're even worse with a gun than Easy Bill. The only reason he got Fanner is he was mad over Bob. The only reason he got Spider was because Spider was facing the light. But you won't get breaks like them. You'd commit *suicide*!"

"We'll see." He was headed for the door.

"Wait, Jimmy! Don't go out and get yourself chawed up. You . . . you didn't get this mad about Bob."

"I didn't like Bob. He was a drunkard and the place is better off without him. But no man is going to malign the name of Easy Bill while I can still reach for iron!"

"Aw, now, Jimmy. If Easy Bill knew—"

"Sure, if he knew he'd go. Greaser Rawkins has got to be dead and buried before Easy Bill can find out. Easy Bill's blind, I tell you. He took three shots to hit a rattler at ten feet. What kind of a fool do you think I am that I'd let him walk into the Greaser's guns?"

"You don't get it," said Rocky. "By accident Easy Bill built a rep as a gunman. He's got to hold that up for the rest of his days. No gunhawk will ever let him forget it. He's a target for every fancy 'slinger. Your killin' the Greaser ain't goin' to help nothin'. It's Barton that'll see this thing through. He wants *Las Piñas*. . . ."

Jimmy was heading for the door, had his hand on it. He turned and gave Rocky a bleak smile. He started out.

Rocky leaned heavily against the table, all the energy gone from him in a flash.

"God, what have I *done?*" he whispered.

He turned to the door again. Suddenly he straightened and strode after Smiling Jimmy, like a tumbleweed in the wake of a twister.

The wrangler was sitting on the top corral bar pensively chewing and accurately spitting. He saw Jimmy coming, noticed something unusual in the foreman's carriage and dropped hurriedly down, chinks flopping like wings as he hit.

Young Jimmy Langman said quietly, "Saddle Mike for me, will you?"

"What's wrong?" demanded the wrangler.

"Saddle Mike," said Smiling Jimmy, as calm as though on his way to a square dance, not his funeral.

Rocky came up as the wrangler loped away.

"What's the sense in this?" demanded Rocky. "Greaser Rawkins will put so much lead in you we'll have to bury you with a crane."

"Well?"

"But what's the sense in that?"

Smiling Jimmy looked toward the deserted veranda of the ranch house.

"I get it. You get killed and Easy Bill . . ." Rocky broke off. "But that don't make sense. I'm going with you."

"All right."

54

Rocky went to locate a mustang for himself. Easy Bill came out on the veranda and looked carefully at the corral. He could not see who was out there and he stepped off and began to slouch toward the corral.

"It's me," said Jimmy.

"Going someplace?"

"They reported some steers down in the valley. I'm going to drive them back."

"Okay," said Easy Bill. "I'd go but I feel kind of tired."

Rocky and the wrangler came back, leading horses. Jimmy swung up and jabbed his toe into his stirrup, looking down at Easy Bill.

"So long," said Jimmy.

"S'long," said Easy Bill. "See you at supper."

Jimmy did not answer. He and Rocky started down the slope at a jogging trot. Jimmy looked back once and waved but Easy Bill, though looking straight at him, did not see.

Chapter Eight

TWILIGHT was blue and restful over quiet *Las Piñas.* The smoke from Easy Bill's pipe drifted out to match the evening. Easy Bill had been sitting there for hours, leaning comfortably back in his chair, eyes closed, listening for the return of Jimmy Langman and Rocky.

He thought it strange that Rocky would go off and leave the pack saddles to Ching the cook, but he had not worried very much about it.

He lifted his head and took the pipe out of his mouth, listening. Far off a running horse was coming up the hills toward the ranch, coming fast.

The sound became a rolling rattle, broken as the horse stumbled on the rough trail in, but growing louder and louder second by second.

Rocky spurred straight for the veranda and came off of his saddle before his horse had stopped running. He hit the steps so hard with his boots that the wood creaked in protest.

Rocky stood by the pillar looking at Easy Bill.

"The Greaser got Smiling Jimmy."

It was said in such a monotonous voice that Easy Bill did not instantly understand. He took his heels off the rail and came slowly up to tower over Rocky.

"What was that?"

"Jimmy went to Red Butte to get the Greaser. The Greaser got him."

"To Red Butte. But he said . . ."

Rocky's face was a mask of grief. Tears had strung back from his eyes as he rode, to leave two white trails of alkali dust horizontal to his ears.

"I did it," said Rocky. "I did it. I told him the Greaser was talkin' about you today. I told him the Greaser said you was a coward because you wouldn't come to Red Butte. And Jimmy buckled on his gun and went."

"But he didn't tell . . . WHY DIDN'T HE SAY SOMETHING TO ME?"

"He wouldn't."

"How did it happen?"

Easy Bill felt cold all over. His brain was clear but his body was numb.

"Jimmy rode in and said he was looking for the Greaser and he walked inside the Coyote. The Greaser was there at the bar. Jimmy said he'd come for him. Rawkins made Jimmy draw first and then beat him with both guns. Five shots . . ."

"Jimmy's dead!"

"The Greaser . . ."

Easy Bill had stopped listening the instant the news had finally drilled home.

He had no feeling in his hands.

Easy Bill reached out to steady himself on the pillar and had to grope for it. Rocky stepped aside so that Easy Bill would not misgauge and touch him instead. He knew better than to try to guide Easy Bill's hand.

Easy Bill turned toward his door and looked at it for some time. He realized that he still held his pipe and he knocked out a shower of live red dots against the rail.

"Smiling Jimmy Langman . . . dead."

Abruptly Easy Bill came alive.

"Saddle Buster!"

"You goin' to Red Butte?"

Easy Bill did not hear him. There was a roaring in his ears. A red curtain had dropped across his brain. The skin on his face was so tight it pulled his lips back from his teeth.

He walked toward the door and groped angrily for the latch. He stepped through across the skin rugs and got his hat from an elk horn by the fireplace.

He stopped then and took his Colt from its holster. Breaking out the cylinder he dumped the cartridges into his hand and looked at them. They were a faint metallic blur to him as he fumbled to put them back.

He heard Buster coming up outside, heard another horse for Rocky.

Easy Bill went to the door, jamming down the Colt and picking up his quirt.

At the steps he shoved a foot in a stirrup and swung aboard.

The quirt cracked against Buster's flank. He leaped ahead and the spurs dug deep.

Splitting the wind and darkness, Buster headed downhill at a dead run.

Chapter Nine

GEORGE BARTON was sitting alone over a drink at a table in the back of the Coyote Saloon. He gnawed ceaselessly upon a tattered cigar and watched the noisy crowd of punchers around the faro table.

Greaser Rawkins was in the crowd, not as noisy as the rest. He did not have to be. When he moved as though to go backwards the path was instantly clear. When he stretched out his hand drinks were put magically into it. When he said something the assemblage made sure whether it was funny or serious and then either laughed or shook their heads at such profound wisdom as the most prudent course presented itself.

Greaser Rawkins was running low on cash, which was strange because the faro dealer was very attentive to the Greaser's winnings. But the Greaser thought he needed money to break the bank and he decided he would have it.

He swaggered through a wonderfully clear lane toward George Barton.

"Barton," said the Greaser, seating himself across the board, "I need money. Say another two hundred on account."

"You haven't killed Easy Bill Gates yet."

"Hell, ain't I done everything I could? After what happened today, that gent will burn up the trail. You sure that runt with the beard was part of *Las Piñas*?"

"That was Rocky Leonard," said Barton gruffly. "He took it back to Gates. Don't worry."

"Then the killing is in the very near future," said the Greaser. "How about two hundred on account?"

"I don't know if I'll even let you kill him," said Barton. "It'll be too easy. I ought to do it myself."

"I didn't know you was handy with a shootin' iron."

"No. Well, I used to be pretty good and don't you forget it." Barton looked at the Greaser and then began to laugh long and soundlessly.

"What's the matter with you?" snapped Rawkins.

"I was laughing at you," said Barton.

The Greaser instantly was up. His hand was going back toward his right-hand Colt.

"Sit down!" ordered Barton. "Don't be so damned touchy."

The Greaser sat down and Barton started laughing again. The Greaser stood it as long as he could but finally that wheezing, asthmatic chortle wore into him.

"Damn you, what you laughing at?"

"You," said Barton, again. "I'm laughing at the peerless gunslinger Greaser Rawkins, the man who never misses and knows no fear."

"What's so funny?" said the Greaser in a deadly monotone.

"You tried to get Easy Bill Gates with a rifle but you said he spotted you first and shot three times. Did he come close to you?"

The Greaser knew the better part of valor was lying. "Sure."

"You wouldn't twist the truth, would you?"

"You think I'd lie?" spat the Greaser in a rage.

"Sure you'd lie," said Barton. "I happen to know that Easy Bill couldn't have come within a mile of you."

"How the hell do you know that?"

Barton started laughing again, tears running down his fat cheeks and hanging in his walrus mustache, with never a sound from him.

Finally he got control of himself and looked long at the jittery, poisonous Greaser Rawkins.

"Because," said Barton, hardly able to talk he was laughing so hard without sound, "because *Easy Bill Gates has been blind for two months!*"

The Greaser's thin eyes popped wide and black. His jaw sagged a little and then, suddenly he got the joke. He slapped his leg and began to shout with laughter.

Presently they quieted down enough to talk.

"He still might be dangerous," said the Greaser.

"How could he hit anything?" chortled Barton.

"That's so."

"Look here. He'll be in shortly or I miss my guess. Can you keep your mouth shut about this?"

"Sure."

"All right. The man who kills Easy Bill gets himself a rep right then. I used to be some handy with a gun. I'm good enough to jab one into a man's ribs and pull the trigger. I give you double pay and I kill him."

"All right."

"When he comes in, the room will clear. I walk up bold

as brass and start talking to him. Then you draw over here against the wall and when he turns to face you—you make some noise about it—I haul out and plug him."

"Sure. It's a good idea."

"Gettin' *Las Piñas* after that will be easy going. I save my stock and you get yourself a good job with me."

"Okay. Sounds all right."

They had a drink on it and then another. The contents in the bottle sagged lower and lower but the stuff had no visible effect upon either of the men. They were too keyed up, too interested in the project at hand.

About ten o'clock a horse was heard thundering up the dark street.

Rawkins sat up and Barton unbuttoned his coat. They exchanged a wide glance.

The horse came to an abrupt stop outside the Coyote. Saddle creaked and two boots hit the ground. The steps creaked under the onslaught of fast steps. The doors crashed inward.

Easy Bill Gates stood against the outer darkness, eyes raking the room before him.

The Coyote was as silent as a church on Monday. Then a whisper like a growing wind devil curled down along the bar.

"It's Easy Bill."

"Easy Bill Gates!"

"EASY BILL GATES COMIN' AFTER RAWKINS!"

The room began to move in a swift blur of chinks and checkered shirts. The side door crashed open under the onslaught of the stampede to get out.

The back door was full and then empty.

The room was still again.

Halfway between the door and the back table hung wraiths of cigarette smoke, drifting in the crosscurrents of the recently disturbed air. Cards were strewn out of the faro box. Stacks of chips were awry on the deserted tables. A line of full and half-full glasses stood in disarray on the bar.

A face came to the front window, framed in a broken sash.

Easy Bill still stood in the door. He was cold inside but his brain was hot as a blacksmith's forge, fanned by the words "Jimmy Langman. Jimmy Langman."

Barton got carefully to his feet and walked slowly forward. Easy Bill saw him and recognized him by his bulk. The Greaser slid up away from his chair and crept down along the wall to get on Bill's left.

Easy Bill did not see the Greaser. He looked at Barton with hard hatred.

"Where is Greaser Rawkins?"

Barton was still coming carefully up.

Easy Bill stepped another pace inside and the doors swung to on their hinges, passing and repassing each other as they settled down.

Barton stopped ten feet from Easy Bill.

An electric stillness gripped Red Butte.

Easy Bill heard a chair rattle against the wall. He whirled in that direction. A foggy shape was there. An evil, vulturelike form.

Easy Bill faced back to Barton. He knew instantly what Barton knew about him. He knew instantly that he was caught between a cross-fire. Rawkins against the wall, Barton before him.

But none of that made any difference to Easy Bill. He was nothing but a hand and a gun.

The Greaser was coming forward again. Something glinted in his hand. Two sharp clicks of a cocking Colt rapped in the silence.

Barton abruptly sidestepped and drew.

Easy Bill's hand went down and came up.

Three shots crashed.

Easy Bill lurched back, ducking into a crouch. He had fired straight ahead but nothing was happening.

The blue haze of drifting smoke made sight more difficult than ever.

Easy Bill held back the hammer.

Barton was standing like a statue. His gun hand started up again.

Easy Bill let his hammer fall. The Colt jolted up and back, ribboning smoke and flame across the ten feet.

Barton's gun started slowly down. Barton came a pace forward, the Colt clattered to the floor.

Something moved against the wall.

Greaser Rawkins was standing there, a look of amazement stamped upon his scarred face. He took a step sideways, back to the wall. One hand was tugging at the butt of his left gun.

Easy Bill ducked back again, still in a crouch. He blasted three quick shots toward the Greaser but he did not see them throwing scraps of paper out of the calendar five feet to the Greaser's right.

Rawkins dropped his arm. He took another step sideways. He sucked in a loud, whistling breath.

Abruptly he went down, leather creaking, spurs jingling, and then everything was still and the blue haze drifted serenely if acridly up toward the flaring kerosene lamps.

Easy Bill looked down at Barton. He could not see Barton's expression but he could see the spatter of blood on his lips. It was too big to miss.

Hesitantly Easy Bill paced forward toward Rawkins. The gunman's back was uppermost. Half the right side was torn away.

Easy Bill slowly turned to the door. He carefully slipped his gun into its holster and stepped ahead, hand out to tell him when he reached the swinging wings.

Rocky suddenly had hold of his arm, leading him out and down the steps.

Easy Bill climbed up on Buster.

What he could see of the night was spinning. A terrible nausea overpowered him as his anger drained away and left him burned out and sick.

Rocky had Buster's reins.

They went down the deserted street, paying no heed to the faces pressed against glass everywhere.

"Barton's dead," whispered Easy Bill. "Rawkins is dead. I . . . I can't understand. . . . I couldn't see. . . ."

"Take your time, Easy Bill," said Rocky with a smile.

"They'd be cheering you back there if they had the nerve. You got Fanner and then Spider and now Rawkins. Unless you go looking for it, no trouble will ever come your way again. You got the reputation. You're a *killer*."

Easy Bill grinned—or tried to grin. He felt too sick about Jimmy. He listened to Buster's hoofs hitting slowly under him.

Into the sound came another. A horse was trotting behind them.

Wasn't it over yet?

Easy Bill turned restively in his saddle. A blurry rider was coming up. A hand reached out from the shadow and shook Bill's arm.

"Good going," said the shadow.

Easy Bill almost fell off his horse. "JIMMY!"

Jimmy Langman was smiling again. He held Easy Bill's arm for a moment before he dropped it.

Easy Bill felt as though he had been dumped into one of his icy mountain streams. He looked up at the sky and saw white, dancing dots which were crystal stars.

Rocky Leonard dragged back and came around on Bill's right, giving Jimmy a sharp prod with the butt of his quirt. Hurriedly Jimmy slipped his .44 Winchester off the crook of his arm and down into the boot.

Easy Bill had not noticed.

"Sorry," said Jimmy. "We knew there was only one thing to do. Get you mad again. Barton's dead. Nobody will have nerve enough to bother you again."

"Sure," grinned Easy Bill, feeling better than he had for a

long time. "Sure, Jimmy. I understand. . . . That is, almost everything. I can guess at the rest."

They walked their horses slowly through the cool night and the lights behind them grew too small to see.

Back in Red Butte, the populace began to arrange for the double funeral of Barton and Greaser Rawkins. They went about it joyously and the name of Easy Bill was loud and happy on every tongue.

There were no ballistics experts in Red Butte.

Ruin at Rio Piedras

Chapter One

A storm cloud of angry dust boiled up the road to the main ranch of the INT, and just before it could be seen two lathered bays, manes flying, heads pumping and hoofs thundering through the white dust.

Dawson, the general manager, came erect in his wicker chair on the veranda and stared with wonder, his tobacco-stained mouth agape and his boots planted upon the planking. A puncher down by the corral yipped, "It's Old Man Tanner!" But Dawson didn't need that information. Only one madman drove like that on such a day. Only one man could afford to wear out horses in so spendthrift a fashion.

The buggy careened into the yard and Old Man Tanner jumped to his feet and leaped down, making the buggy sway as though it had been buffeted by a hurricane. A young lady, a lovely young blond lady, Nancy Tanner, who was most dear to the old man's heart, was glad of Dawson's aid in getting her to earth. She was dazed with so much dust and sunlight. But Old Man Tanner wasn't thinking about his daughter's health. He had driven like a thunderstorm and he arrived like a blast of lightning.

There was nothing small about Tanner. He was a colossus in everything including the INT, which was so big that men said its removal out of Texas wouldn't leave much more to the state than a dotted borderline. Tanner himself stood six feet three and weighed two hundred and forty pounds. He had the face of a Saint Bernard and the eye of a lobo. His voice at a whisper, the punchers swore, could be heard for thirty miles on a wet day.

"Place looks like a goddamned cemetery!" roared Tanner. "So this is the way you run things when I'm not around?"

"I just came in," said Dawson, timidly.

"Don't lie to me! You haven't been off this porch all day. Well? Where are the two thousand prime beeves I wired you to roundup day before yesterday?" And he angrily ranged his piercing eyes over the plains about the ranch.

"There . . . there aren't any here at the main ranch," gulped Dawson. "I had to send out to Rio Piedras—but they'll be here tomorrow," he added hastily.

"Tomorrow! By God, they'd better had be. Do you know that I'll have cars on the siding at noon? And I can't hold those cars more than twenty-four hours unless I use them! Can't I depend on anybody? Who is in charge of Rio Piedras?"

"Jim Lowrie," shivered Dawson. "You sent him out there yourself, remember? You . . . that is . . . you exiled—"

"Jim Lowrie!" cried Tanner. "Tumbleweed Lowrie! Why, you blithering fool! Do you think for ten seconds that that young squirt could get two cows together, much less two thousand? And here I am depending on Lowrie! Dawson, this ought to cost you your job. Do you know what I'm up against?"

"No, sir."

"They're shutting down on me, that's what. They won't

extend my paper. They're trying to wreck me. And I got a market. I dug up a market at this time of year for two thousand beeves, two-year-old stuff, and nothing more or less than that. The railroad won't hold those cars without cash and I can't get cash. Those cattle at the very latest should be started from Rio Piedras by tomorrow noon to get to Bowie by dawn the day after. And that'll take some driving! And further, I'll bet your swell-headed young Lowrie hasn't even begun to get them together."

Nancy protested. "He's not as bad as all that, Daddy."

"Bah!" snorted Tanner. "He shoots up Bowie and goes to jail. He gets drunk and tries to make love to my daughter—"

"He wasn't drunk," said Nancy.

"Never mind. He had a nerve. A no-good puncher without money or prospects trying to marry himself a fortune. A gunslingin' yap all bent for the owl-hoot. He's no good, I tell you. Say! I sent him to Rio Piedras because that was the worst place I could put him. But who the hell made him foreman there?"

"Well," said Dawson miserably, "I . . . I didn't have anybody else. Conner quit and Lowrie was next in line out there. . . ."

"Oh, God," said Tanner in mock anguish, "can't anybody ever do anything right? Dawson! Saddle a Piedmont. I am going out there and take charge of that myself. It's a matter of life and death. On that depends the whole INT. If I could get those beeves closer—"

"You can't," said Dawson. "All the two-year-olds were shunted—"

"Don't tell me about my own ranch!" stormed Tanner,

starting to stamp up the steps. But at the first hard bang of his boot on wood, he let out a groan and grabbed for his foot and stood there swearing.

Dawson and Nancy supported him. "It's his gout," said Nancy to Dawson. "The doctor told him not to get angry."

"Lowrie," Tanner was sobbing. "Tumbleweed Lowrie. I'll hear that name in my sleep. Every time something happens, it's Tumbleweed Lowrie. It's your fault!" he snapped at Nancy. "You wouldn't let me fire him when I caught him kissing you. By God . . ."

"Please," said Nancy.

"I'll send a man out to Rio Piedras right away. And maybe by tomorrow morning you can ride out there yourself. It's not an easy trip, Mr. Tanner." Dawson shouted, "Conroy!"

A moment later a dark-clothed man with slick hair and two gleaming gold teeth came ingratiatingly around the end of the ranch house where he had quite obviously been for some time. He held his Stetson in his hand and bowed.

"I am sorry you are not feeling well," said Blackie Conroy to Tanner. "You owe it to the ranch to take better care of yourself, sir. Ah, good afternoon, Miss Tanner. I hope you are well?"

Nancy looked away but Tanner's face relaxed a trifle. "Oh, hello, Conroy. It's my gout."

"If there is anything I can do . . ." began Conroy anxiously.

"There's something you can do," said Tanner. "You can ride out to Rio Piedras and take over from that young fool Lowrie. Conroy, if we don't get those beeves into Bowie before day after tomorrow, I'm a ruined man. I'm glad there's somebody I can trust around here," and he glared at Dawson.

"I was afraid something ill would come of appointing Lowrie, sir," said Conroy, looking sad. "But I'll do what I can to remedy the situation."

Very businesslike, Conroy replaced his hat, adjusted the chin thong and then strode with jingling spurs around the end of the ranch house where he had tied his horse, well knowing the sequence of events beforehand. He made a dashing picture as he hurled himself to saddle and went with slashing quirt down the road toward Rio Piedras.

"There's somebody I can trust at least," said Tanner with a sigh. "Sometimes, Nancy, I don't think you've got good sense."

The girl looked after Conroy as though she had seen a rattlesnake.

Chapter Two

S HORTLY before dusk, Blackie Conroy spurred across the boundary of the Rio Piedras section. As the INT furnished him his string, he was not sparing the quirt even though the ground had become uneven. Here was a line of hills which rose gradually from the prairie to fall off again into the Rio Grande. The country was desolate and tortuous and so was not regarded with any favor by the INT riders. The grass was good and there was water. But there were also badlands too labyrinthine to be mapped and into them cattle were wont to lose themselves with determination. And, what was more important to a puncher, there was only one lone town near the ranch buildings and that was an excuse for a pueblo, mired down in the Mexican sands across the river and too lazy to move itself elsewhere. An assignment to duty in Rio Piedras was synonymous with banishment and, when news of such an assignment reached ears, the question was always asked, "What did he do?" But for all that, it was good cattle country—when men across the border were quiet.

Blackie, scorching the trail, energized by the tidings he looked forward to giving out, still found time to note a strange fact. For the last two miles he had seen only one animal and he was an old longhorn outlaw scorned these many years as beef.

And when Blackie got through the ragged pass and dropped down along the sluggish brown Rio Grande to head northwest toward the ranch buildings, he had still to see a good beef. Usually this stretch was very populous with cattle and Blackie had a bad moment, thinking that Tumbleweed Lowrie might have come through after all with that swift roundup.

Darkness came and he was still six miles short of the ranch headquarters. He laid on more heavily with the quirt, anxious to discover the truth. The river fled by on his left and the uneven trail pitched up and down beneath his mount's flying hoofs. So intent was he upon speed that the first shot which came to him from afar was totally lost upon him. But a second and third made him hastily drag rein and send his mount pawing air. When the bronc had settled to earth, another shot sounded somewhere in the hills to Blackie's right. Neck-reining, he spurred up a dry gully, alertly watching the blackness ahead.

A ribbon of sparks ripped the ebony and a belated report rolled around the hills. Blackie threw himself off his horse and advanced on foot with great care.

Abruptly, straight ahead, a Colt blazed. The hot snap of the bullet was close beside Blackie's head.

"Hey! Quit it!" yowled Blackie. "I'm Conroy!"

"Come on," called a man up in the rocks, immediately firing in the other direction.

Cautiously, Blackie crawled up beside him. It was Tumbleweed. In the calmest of moments this young man had the air of violence about him and just now his eyes were hot as coals. One got the impression that he was about to explode like a bomb, so difficult was it for him to contain his bursting vitality. His lean, roughly handsome face shone in the gloom and he snapped down with his Colt as though he had to throw the slug with his own strength.

"Whatcha waitin' for?" demanded Tumbleweed. "Charlie Bates and two men're up there in those rocks! Smoke up!"

"Bates?" said Blackie with a start. "Why . . . why, that's impossible. The Rangers got him last year!"

"If they did, his ghost is mighty handy with a brandin' iron. Sling lead from here while I inch around and get in back of them."

"Y-You mean you're going to take all three of them? Wh-Wh-Where's your outfit?"

"You scared or somethin'?" demanded Tumbleweed.

"N-N-N-No, of course not," said Blackie.

"Keep shootin'. They think I'm alone. That gray rock up there . . . see it? They're behind that." Thereupon Tumbleweed slid out of hiding and sped down the slope into the gully to turn left and begin to work his way upward.

Blackie fired now and then without any particular target. His head was too busy for him to give much thought to marksmanship.

"Charlie Bates, is it?" he muttered to himself. "Oh, this is sweet. This is lovely. That rustler wouldn't leave a calf behind him. And everybody thinks he's dead and all the Rio Piedras cattle are gone. . . . Mr. Lowrie, you may be handy with your tongue and hell with your guns, but this is one time when you picked on the wrong man." And through his mind passed the memory of a time, three months gone, when

81

Tumbleweed Lowrie had pitched him into a horse trough to the amusement of all Bowie. What business had it been of Tumbleweed's that Blackie Conroy had boasted a certain affair with one Nancy Tanner? Especially since it was pretty apparent from this exiling that Tumbleweed himself hadn't been slow to make up to her.

"Charlie Bates," he muttered again with glee. "And with this clean sweep he'll be heading for Mexico and there won't be a thing to show that Tumbleweed Lowrie hasn't been fattening his own . . ."

A series of shattering reports sounded behind the gray pinnacle. The hill was alight with powder flame and through that intermittent flashing sprinted a man. There was no doubt about his identity. The faint glimpse had told Blackie that this was Bates in all his silver conchas. And though Bates had been a good target in that moment, Blackie Conroy had not fired.

A moment later a horse clattered away in the darkness. From the pinnacle came a halloo. "Conroy! Why the hell didn't you stop him?"

Blackie didn't answer. Taking it for granted that Tumbleweed had things in hand higher up, he toiled up the hill. In the darkness two men were sprawled, sightless eyes staring up at the bright diamond stars. They were Mexicans and so did not particularly interest Conroy.

"I had him!" cried Tumbleweed. "They thought I was still down there. And all you had to do was shoot and we'd of gotten Bates! Damn it, I've trailed these gents for six hours trying to get up on them and you have to spoil it all! I ought to make hash out of you!"

Conroy stepped back a little. Men didn't stand up to this youngster if they could help it.

"I didn't see him until it was too late," said Blackie.

Tumbleweed snorted in derision. He collected the guns of the dead men and then went through their pockets to try to uncover evidence. But their pockets were empty.

"It's too dark now," said Tumbleweed, staring forlornly into the blackness. He sighed deeply as though all the world was upon his back. "Come on, I'm hungry." He strode down the gully to his horse and Blackie, in sudden shock, looked around for his own.

"I cut their broncs loose. Looks like we're ridin' double," said Tumbleweed. "Serves you right for not shootin' that devil."

Blackie climbed up to the bronc's rump and they headed out for the ranch.

"What are you doin' up here?" said Tumbleweed. "This place is bad enough already. Cattle missin', nothing to drink but river water, not even a can of peaches for forty miles, a crew that growls all day about their hard luck, and now you."

Conroy was about to state his business and then something prompted him to withhold it.

"I'm taking over," said Blackie.

"I don't know what the hell you'll take over," said Tumbleweed crossly. "No cattle, no men. Damned few supplies. There's a jug of molasses in camp. Maybe you can take that over."

"No men?" said Conroy.

"Of course not!" snapped Tumbleweed so violently that Conroy didn't want to speak again. The presence of Charlie Bates in Rio Piedras would of course quell stronger men than the INT men who had been sent here. They had not been particularly desirable, any of them. And it was more than likely that some of them had teamed up with Bates.

At long last they reached the dark ranch. The 'dobe buildings had a weary, crumbling air about them and a shutter groaned and banged in the night wind.

Tumbleweed stabled his buckskin and then led the way to the main building. Inside he lighted a lamp which showed up the racked guns on the wall and the total absence of other adornment. The chairs were crates with the nails driven in and the table was a dry-goods box.

Tumbleweed immediately fell to work cleaning his guns and Conroy, by common consent, threw some pancakes together. Dinner was ready and the guns were clean at the same time and they sat down across from each other, with the lamp between them. They were silent because they had never had anything in common and Conroy was too occupied with his own problem and Tumbleweed too concerned about the escape of Bates to think of anything else.

When they had finished, Tumbleweed looked a long time at Conroy. "I suppose they want me back at the main ranch. But I'm not going. I got ideas about Bates. Must be plenty of stock hidden out somewhere in the badlands. The Mexicans tell me 'most everything and they ain't seen nothin' cross the

Rio Grande. God!" he exclaimed suddenly bringing his fist down on the box, "to think I almost had him!"

"How long has this been going on?" said Conroy.

"Hell, about three weeks to my knowledge. Didn't Jim Fallon tell you anything when I sent him back? He didn't show up here again and I supposed—"

"Fallon hasn't been back," said Conroy.

"Probably dry-gulched then," said Tumbleweed. "That's the trouble with this place. Always all hell breakin' loose and people get to thinkin' that the bad news ain't important, there's so much of it. Boy, I'm tellin' you. The main ranch is going to be a relief after this!"

"Yeah, I suppose so," said Conroy, still busy with the problem of getting some *vaqueros* over the line and throwing at least an excuse for a herd together for the Bowie drive. Tumbleweed might be irresponsible but he had so damned much energy that he couldn't be trusted. If the message about the two thousand had never reached him or if he had forgotten about it—which seemed to be apparent in his bandit hunt—it was all the same to Old Man Tanner. Conroy had his doubts about Tanner's true sentiments towards Tumbleweed. The cattleman usually roared like a gored longhorn at a man when he liked him the most. But there wouldn't be any doubt about that now. Probably Tumbleweed would go galloping off to pick up Bates' trail in the morning and that would leave an opportunity to grab some *vaqueros* from Santa Maria and sling a herd together the best he could. There would still be time, though he wouldn't be able to be choosy. There were

85

always plenty of beeves up in the hills behind Rio Piedras, bandits or no bandits. And then up would come Tanner to find Conroy, the hero of the occasion. . . . It was very pleasant and Conroy smiled.

"What are you grinnin' at?" said Tumbleweed.

Conroy started. "Nothing."

"Never saw a man so pleased about 'nothing,'" said Tumbleweed, getting to his feet. He stretched and yawned, sinuous as a panther. "Guess I'll turn in. Got to start ridin' early tomorrow."

Conroy smiled again, watching Tumbleweed head for the bunkhouse. He would still have to take precautions to put this over right. Tumbleweed wasn't a man to monkey with if he thought he was being framed. And Tumbleweed was the biggest stumbling block on the road to a certain destination Conroy had in mind. Nancy wouldn't care a lot for a man who had apparently brought her father so near the brink of ruin.

Chapter Three

TUMBLEWEED LOWRIE slid out of his blankets a full two hours before dawn. His buckskin shirt was cold as he slid into it and laced it up the front. His chinks, scarred with hard usage, were now ripped from his work in the rocks the night before. Dressed, he did not look very ornamental, since he did not bother about shaving and dumped his face ears deep into the river in lieu of his usual morning bath. But then Tumbleweed was a man of contradictions. He could speak perfect English if he wished. He could be the worst rowdy in the world or he could be a model for the Bowie parson (which he wasn't). And in his war bag were clothes of such flash and color that the Mexicans called him Pretty Shadow—when he wasn't listening.

He was not what one might call a reliable citizen, since he even forgot this morning that Blackie Conroy was in camp. So intent was he on picking up the trail where he had lost it that he bothered about nothing but coffee. And then, cramming his pockets full of biscuit and slinging his canteen over his shoulder, he went out to the corrals and got himself a fresh mount.

His eyes were mirrors of his moods, ranging in color from gray through green to bright blue, depending on whether or not he was bored. He had been bored for some time on the Rio Piedras but now his glance was like aquamarine, electric enough to be powered by a dynamo.

Through the darkness he made his way back to the place where he had cornered Charlie Bates. The sun came up to gild the Rio Grande and crimson-paint the rocks. Great lumps of sage made purple splotches on the hills.

He found the tracks and not until then did he recall Conroy. But then it made no difference. Conroy was all soft-soap and no guts. Hell of a man to take over Rio Piedras where desertions were many, grouches were abundant and deaths most frequent. But it served Conroy right. And to the pocket of his chinks went Tumbleweed's long hand to touch a white glove given to him those many months before. For a moment Tumbleweed felt weary. It didn't seem as though he would ever do anything more than kick around through the hills and chase cattle. What chance did a man ever have to come up in this feudal world unless he was loose enough with a branding iron (which Tumbleweed was not)? Once upon a time he had rolled from the Mississippi to the Pacific in perfect content. A month in one place had been too long. What chemistry had happened in him which made him look with jaundiced eye upon such a purposeless life? He touched the glove again and then buttoned the pocket down.

Pushing his flat-brimmed Stetson back until the thong was taut against his chin, he examined the marks in the trail so that he could identify the horse through the errors in the shoes in case the trail got tangled. He had high hopes of coming on his quarry before many miles, since that mount had done sixty-nine miles the day before at a fast pace. Conroy was a bronc killer.

He mounted, noting that the trail swung down along the river, and followed it with practiced eye at a trot. Only the one horse had been this way in two days and so it was not hard to do. After two miles of swift going, the trail branched sharply left and started up into a slashed and gutted badland. Tumbleweed eyed the hills with care and loosened his gun in its holster. Other trails had taken him toward this spot and he knew that Bates must have six or seven men with him at his camp. This stretch was a catch-all. Murderers and thieves escaping both American and Mexican justice lodged here to prey upon the border. The ravines were deep and the valleys sudden. It was possible to use any of these canyon walls as forts. A regiment could not dislodge a dozen from such a place.

Before this, when he had traced missing cattle, the trail had always led to this section. And now Bates himself had come this way. Yesterday when he had picked up Bates in Santa Maria, a Mexican had mentioned a valley which had much water and grass. Maybe that was the place.

Tumbleweed spurred forward on the alert, not knowing from what quarter a slug might come. And not caring too much since this was the first excitement he had had in many weeks.

Deeper he wove his way through the canyons, watching the kaleidoscopic layers of rock and gravel bend and twist on either side. Each sage might hide a gunner, each cliff might boast a lookout. And they knew Tumbleweed all too well. Tumbleweed had a habit of being known.

He was nearing the mentioned valley and still on Bates' trail. Ahead he saw two great walls rising into the yellow sky, making an opening less than twenty feet across.

"Nope," said Tumbleweed, reining in behind a boulder. "Not this morning, gents."

He backed out around a bend of the canyon and then turned to quirt his mount up a long slope which led to a ridge as flat as though it had been chopped off with a knife.

Just before he reached the top he stopped and dismounted, tethering his mount to a clump of sage. Afoot he went to the rim and scouted the surface. All was quiet there, but he made no skyline target of himself. On hands and knees he crawled along the course which he had paralleled below. At long last he came to a position from which he could observe the valley.

He gave a small sigh of relief and pleasure. The cup-like depression, carpeted with long grass, was colored reddish brown by the cattle it contained.

"So," said Tumbleweed in relief, "this is the place. Damned if you haven't pretty near cleaned out Rio Piedras at that!"

A small cluster of 'dobe huts, once occupied by Indians, had been appropriated by Bates and his men. Tumbleweed took a small glass from his shirt pocket and focused it.

"Fallon!" he said in amazement. "And Dodd!"

So that was the answer to a smooth-working rustling crew. Fallon and Dodd had known all the answers. And that was the reason no help had come.

Tumbleweed cursed his lack of men. It seemed impossible to do anything against the eight down there. But he had waited so long for this moment that now he could not restrain

RUIN AT RIO PIEDRAS

· R U I N   A T   R I O   P I E D R A S ·

himself. He inched back out of sight and then with rapid
steps began a circuit of the valley just below the rim.

himself. He inched back out of sight and then with rapid steps began a circuit of the valley just below the rim.

The going was hard and the day was hot, but Tumbleweed with something to do which interested him was a stranger to terror or fatigue. It was only when he was bored that he had no drive.

An hour and a half of work brought him to a spot above the 'dobe huts built up the cliff. He lay there looking down. The men were taking it easy in the shade.

But Tumbleweed wouldn't be stopped. He edged along the rimrock until he discovered one of the chimneys, left by softer stone weathering out of the harder mass. It was about four feet across, open on one side to the valley. And it went straight down for a long, long way. Tumbleweed took a deep breath and started. By bracing his back against one side and his boots against the other, he could hunch his way earthward slowly but certainly.

He was scraped on back and shins when he finally landed but he did not greatly care—in fact, in his excitement he felt no pain whatever.

The back of a 'dobe hut was about thirty feet away. The stones were thick on this slope which led down. On his stomach, using stones for cover, Tumbleweed crossed the open space.

He came to the back of the hut and peered through the ragged curtain into a bare room. There was nothing here and he moved on to the next.

And there he found why he had not seen Bates. The man was lying at length on a pile of blankets very peacefully snoring.

Cat-footed, Tumbleweed went through the window with never a sound. He quietly drew his Colt and knelt beside Bates. The cold muzzle rested against the outlaw's side.

"Wake up easy," cautioned Tumbleweed.

Bates lurched up to his elbows, one hand gripping the butt of a gun. He was wide awake on the instant and did not try to draw. "You!" said Bates.

"Yeah, me. Wanna take a ride?"

Bates scratched his greasy beard and grinned. "Don't make me laugh, fellah. I got eight men that'd come if I let out one chirp."

"But not before you was awful dead," said Tumbleweed.

Bates looked at the puncher's face and then decided not to yell. "Well," he challenged, "now that you've got me, what the hell are you going to do about it?"

Tumbleweed took the outlaw's gun and stepped to the door. Hidden from the view of the lounging men were four horses, saddled up in case the cattle had to be handled in a hurry. He came back to Bates. "Get your duds off, brother. You probably got every known brand of varmints, but the INT ain't going to lose fifty thousand bucks in cattle if I can help it."

"What you going to do?" gaped Bates.

"Strip," said Tumbleweed, beginning to shuck out of his own clothes. He threw the shirt to Bates who put it on, and then followed chinks and jeans.

Presently they were dressed in each other's clothes. Bates was really worried by now. "You goin' to get me killed?"

"Never can tell," said Tumbleweed, buttoning up Bates' red shirt over his own chest. "But I'm at least givin' you a fair chance to go on livin'! Now walk out there slow and get on one of them hosses. I'm right behind you and the first move you make, you're dead!"

Bates hung back but he took another look at Tumbleweed's face and at last moved through the door. He mounted, shaking a little with uncertainty.

"Now," said Tumbleweed, "you'll have a chance to get away from me if you can make it. Just keep ridin' like hell straight ahead for the pass and then down to the river. I got a better horse here so don't get too fancy an idea. And mister, you better ride! Your boys pretty good shots?"

Bates didn't answer. He was white beneath the broad brim of Tumbleweed's hat. Tumbleweed's quirt cracked on the other mount's flank.

Bates started out, knowing he couldn't help himself, by digging spur and lashing his mount like fury. But for all that, when he rounded the end of the huts, a hundred yards and better from his lounging men, he forgot himself to shout, "It's Lowrie! Get him!" Bullets cracked on the instant and Bates remembered and dug spur again. Tumbleweed, with an encouraging wave to the men, went hell for leather after the apparent Tumbleweed.

Bullets cracked for a moment and then stopped, since it was occurring to the outlaws that they might hit "Bates."

One behind the other, the two horsemen raced for the pass. A guard leaped up ahead of them and beheld the buckskin shirt and flat hat in advance and the red shirt speeding behind. The guard threw his Winchester to his shoulder and fired. Bates ducked, screaming curses at his man. He tried to draw in but behind him Tumbleweed fired. Bates spurred ahead through the pass, the puncher so close upon him that the guard confused them and stopped firing.

The guard glanced up as "Bates" went by but "Bates" did an astonishing thing. He reined in suddenly and grabbed the rifle away.

"Tumbleweed Lowrie!" cried the guard in recognition.

"Tell your pals to clear out fast," said Tumbleweed. "I'll have thirty men up here in half an hour to wipe you out if you ain't gone. And don't try takin' no stock with you."

But there wasn't any use trying to tell the men anything. They were mounted now and lunging over the valley floor like a tornado, anxious to be in on the chase.

Tumbleweed hadn't looked for that. He dug spur and shot ahead in pursuit of Bates.

Calling the turns to his captive, Tumbleweed at last reached the river to head northwest. Bates wasn't sure what was going to happen to him. Once he tried to deviate but a shot swerved him back to the trail. And then he heard the men roaring on in pursuit far behind and took courage. He strove to slow down but Tumbleweed's quirt cracked once and Bates was riding a runaway.

Up the bank of the Rio Grande they raced, sending dust writhing up to meet the clouds. Bates now and again slowed his mount and bit by bit the crew behind caught up to pistol range. At that pace they could hope to hit nothing, since they were still avoiding the shooting of "Bates," but the lead cracking high overhead drove Tumbleweed on to greater speed. Now he didn't know where he was going. The ranch would be deserted.

94

The guard glanced up as "Bates" went by but "Bates"
did an astonishing thing. He reined in suddenly
and grabbed the rifle away.

Conroy counted for nothing in a fight. Tumbleweed guessed he'd have to keep on as long as the horses would go and then make a one-man stand of it—which was not very encouraging.

The six miles were swiftly sped at that pace. And then Bates hove into sight of Rio Piedras. Startled he yanked rein and his rearing mount almost took Tumbleweed into the dust. Tumbleweed slashed with his quirt and Bates got started once more.

And then Tumbleweed saw what had stopped the outlaw. They were riding straight into the arms of a crowd of men who stared open-mouthed for an instant.

"Stop these rannies!" bellowed Tumbleweed, weary of riding the hurricane. "They're rustlers!"

The crowd behind were also late in seeing, since Tumbleweed's dust had been a screen. And by the time they got half turned, guns were going furiously at the ranch.

Tumbleweed dropped into the dust to keep from getting a stray. And from his position there he turned to help. But no help was needed. The outlaws would not risk riding back over that flat expanse to the tune of Winchester fire. Three were already down. The others held up their hands and punchers came forward to disarm them.

And then Tumbleweed saw a most peculiar thing. Bates, dressed in the puncher's buckskin, was lying spread-eagled upon the earth. A cry of alarm and grief burst from behind the INT men and forward sprinted Nancy to throw herself down beside the buckskin-clad figure.

"Oh, Tumbleweed!" she cried. "You're . . . HE'S DEAD!"

Tumbleweed stood over her for a moment, watching. Then

he rolled Bates over and Nancy saw the man's face. She stared up into Tumbleweed's laughing blue eyes and with a surge of relief she sprang into his arms.

But she was not there long. Old Man Tanner came thundering up. "Young man," he stormed, "I've got a thing or two to say to you. What the hell is the meaning of this? What's the idea disobeying my orders and not even sending back word that you couldn't get that beef? My whole outfit is hinging upon two thousand cattle and where were you? Where were you? I'll tell you where you were. Out hunting bandits, that's where! Out hunting bandits when I am going to rack and ruin for two thousand beeves! Where are your men?"

"They—"

"I don't blame them for deserting you! I don't blame Fallon and Dodd over there for joining up with Bates! You're . . . you're . . ."

"Wait," said Tumbleweed. "I—"

"Wait, be damned. That's all I do! Why can't you have some responsibility like Conroy? He's trying to get cattle together right now but the range is cleaned. And it's too late! Too late! We'll never make it in time now. They won't hold those cars!"

"Please," said Tumbleweed. "The range is clean because Bates cleaned it. There're about three thousand head over in a valley—"

"A lot of good they'll do us now! Ohhhhhhh, you wretch! Ohhhhh, if there were just some way I could legally have your life! You're worse than Bates. Conroy is worth five—"

"Where is Conroy?" interrupted Tumbleweed. "Hey, you!"

97

Conroy was very cocky now. He stepped forward beside the dead Bates.

"Bates had my clothes on," said Tumbleweed. "And I bet I don't have to look very far to find the man that shot him thinkin' it was me."

"You're crazy," said Conroy, scared nonetheless.

"Too bad it wasn't you!" wept Tanner. "I'm ruined! They'll take the INT! And all for two thousand beeves."

"Oh, I remember," said Tumbleweed. "Two thousand two-year-olds to Bowie. Is that what—?"

"He remembers!" shrieked Tanner. "We're saved! He remembers!" And then he grabbed Tumbleweed's shirt and snatched him close, intending to knock him down. But Tumbleweed was quick even in the grip of that colossus. He stepped on Tanner's foot and the old man screamed and sank down on the earth, holding the gouty offender.

"If you'll shut up a minute," said Tumbleweed, "I'll tell you something of interest. I—"

"To hell with that!" shouted Tanner. "Ain't it enough to ruin me without talking about it too?"

"But your beeves—" began Tumbleweed anew.

"Shut up!" cried Tanner.

"*Your beeves!*" screamed Tumbleweed, "went to Bowie yesterday by the north trail and are probably loaded by now!"

"What?" gaped Tanner.

"I said—"

"I heard you," cried the old man in joy, leaping up, his gout forgotten. He flung his arms about Tumbleweed. "You mean it? You're not lying?"

"Where do you think the men are?" retorted Tumbleweed. "Lots of crew desert from here, but not mine."

"Oh, my boy, my boy!" wept Tanner. "You've saved me from ruin!"

"And I saved you three thousand head up in that valley, too. Don't forget that," said Tumbleweed.

"It's genius," declared Tanner suddenly. "That's what it is, genius!" And then he stumbled over Bates and remembered. His mood got black and he advanced slow and ugly upon Blackie Conroy. "A murderer, eh? So you tried to murder a genius, eh? By God . . ."

But Conroy grabbed a horse, mounted and fled with Tanner still roaring after him. Then the old man turned and smiled and started to embrace Tumbleweed again. But he couldn't.

Tumbleweed was already being embraced.

Story Preview

NOW that you've just ventured through some of the captivating tales in the Stories from the Golden Age collection by L. Ron Hubbard, turn the page and enjoy a preview of *Gun Boss of Tumbleweed*. Join Mart Kincaid, a man who is forced to act as a gunhawk for a man he bitterly hates in order to protect his family . . . at least until he's driven to bring matters to a fiery six-gun showdown.

Gun Boss of Tumbleweed

S OME day, hombre, one of these squeezed-out rancheros is goin' to get past your guns, and when he does, they'll be measurin' you for a sod kimono. And personally, it'll do my heart a world of good to see you skippin' over the red-hot coals of hell."

Mart Kincaid said it with insolence, a wicked flash in his eye. But somehow it was tired, too—tired with the weight of five years on the payroll of Gar Malone, King of the Concha Basin.

The sun was August hot in the searing blue bowl of the Southwest sky, but it wasn't the sun which made Gar Malone jerk his hat lower to hide his eyes.

They sat their horses for a little, on the edge of the trail, neither one of them willing to let it drop without further venom—for they hated each other as the rattlesnake hates the gila, and they had hated each other for a long, long time.

Gar Malone was corpse-thin, hot for gain, killer-ruthless in his sway of range in four hugely unsurveyed counties. His eyes were dark, his teeth were black, there was no light whatever to the flame of thirsty ambition which scorched within him, searing him on to further power, further wealth, further conquest.

He was no coward, Gar Malone, but he knew his man.

"What objections you got? Seems like you're kinda late, Kincaid."

"Sure, sure. I'm the fallen sparrow and my hands ain't fit to touch a decent horse. But they ain't my crimes, Gar Malone."

"Crimes? Why for cripe's sake, what kind of a baby have you turned into? What's criminal in bein' the biggest horn toad in this furnace? What's so damned dirty about shovin' weaklings and peewee stockmen out of the country? Did they invent it? God made it, Kincaid, and it's for the one that can take it and keep it."

"God may have made it," said Mart, "but He sure didn't count on a brand artist comin' along and turnin' it into what it is. There ain't fifty decent people from here to Tumbleweed. It's gettin' kind of monotonous pitchin' into every poor citizen that wants to eat, work and prosper within a hundred miles any direction. I don't object to dirt but I get tired wallerin' in it and pretendin' it's rose petals."

"You goin' to Tumbleweed, or ain't you?" snapped Gar.

"Oh, sure, sure. I'll go to Tumbleweed. I'll knock out the Singing Canyon spread. I'll stand back and let the boys throw lead into honest punchers whose only crime is bein' loyal to a good boss. Sure, I'll do it."

"Now, that's better," said Gar, mollified considerable. "You're the best gun in the state and the gold I pay clinks. But by all that's holy, Kincaid, if I have to go on takin' all this off'n you, you think I'm goin' to forget what I know?"

"Dead men ain't got no memories to speak of at all," said Kincaid.

Gar's dark gaze fastened upon the silver-chased cannons in Kincaid's buscadero belt. His breath went shallow. "Try it, Kincaid. Go ahead and try it. And the Saturday I don't appear in Lawson, Jeb Barly takes the sealed packet out of his bank safe and puts it in the hands of the US deputy marshal. You won't be the only one that will get green-gilled that day. Think twice, gunman. Think twice."

"You ain't panicky, are you?" said Kincaid. His laugh was insolent, without any amusement whatever.

"You think I don't know your fanning? Why do I pay you? And we both know why you go on workin' for me. I need you. You and Gary O'Neil need me alive." Gar's mood changed into pretended lightness and warmth. "I hear," he continued, "that young Gary's ma got herself a new house on her birthday. Now wasn't that just wonderful of you boys? I tell you, it does my heart good."

"You know, hombre," said Mart, "there's times when I just plain itch to let the desert breezes fan gently through yore hide." And as swift as lightning he rolled his guns and slammed four rapid shots into a cast-off canteen beside the trail. The first made it leap into the air, the second, third and fourth rent it apart before it could fall once more.

The first shot Gar had felt in his own flesh. He didn't breathe comfortably until the white powder smoke had drifted well down the trail.

"I guess," said Mart, "that I'll be headin' out for Tumbleweed."

He jerked his pack horse forward and spurred his gray. If he had looked back he would have seen Gar Malone still sitting his bay beside the trail, looking after him with eyes which sought furtively for a way to end this tension and still rule the Concha Basin.

But Mart Kincaid didn't look back. He was in a more than usually bitter mood. At twenty-five, he felt, he should be well on his way toward making a decent man of himself, carving a fine future from this gaudy but fertile desert realm. But who was he? Gar Malone's peacifier. At twenty-five he was Mart Kincaid, general of the forces of Concha Basin's private and personal devil, a man who used him as guns and brains and kept him chained as thoroughly as Gar's big greyhounds, imported from the East to run down and kill wolves.

It was sixty miles as the buzzard soars to Tumbleweed but it was better than twenty-nine more if one connected with the water holes and used the better trails. But Mart was in no hurry and he added six more in a detour past O'Neil's small ranch.

He felt bad and his eyes were turned so far in that as he came through the canyon below the ranch he did not see, there on the narrow trail before him, the six Malone punchers, part of the home ranch crew.

To find out more about *Gun Boss of Tumbleweed* and how you can obtain your copy, go to www.goldenagestories.com.

106

Glossary

STORIES FROM THE GOLDEN AGE *reflect the words and expressions used in the 1930s and 1940s, adding unique flavor and authenticity to the tales. While a character's speech may often reflect regional origins, it also can convey attitudes common in the day. So that readers can better grasp such cultural and historical terms, uncommon words or expressions of the era, the following glossary has been provided.*

alkali: a powdery white mineral that salts the ground in many low places in the West. It whitens the ground where water has risen to the surface and gone back down.

ballistics expert: one who specializes in firearms. Ballistics experts are trained in and responsible for the processing of crime scenes of ballistic-related evidence: examining firearms and tool marks. Every firearm has its own particular characteristics that are carried over onto the cartridge case and the bullet during the firing process, and a ballistics expert can match a bullet that has been fired to the firearm that was used.

barrel tan: to change an animal hide into leather by soaking in a barrel containing a tanning solution.

beeves: plural of *beef*, an adult cow, steer or bull raised for its meat.

brand artist: a rustler, one expert at changing brands.

brimstone: "fire-and-brimstone"; threatening punishment in the hereafter.

buckboard wagon: a four-wheeled wagon of simple construction having a platform fastened directly to the axles with seating attached for the driver.

buscadero belt: a broad belt for two guns, one on either side.

chinks: short leather chaps (leggings), usually fringed and stopping just below the knee, worn over the pants for protection.

Colt: a single-action, six-shot cylinder revolver, most commonly available in .45- or .44-caliber versions. It was first manufactured in 1873 for the Army by the Colt Firearms Company, the armory founded by American inventor Samuel Colt (1814–1862) who revolutionized the firearms industry with the invention of the revolver. The Colt, also known as the Peacemaker, was also made available to civilians. As a reliable, inexpensive and popular handgun among cowboys, it became known as the "cowboy's gun" and a symbol of the Old West.

concha: a disk, traditionally of hammered silver and resembling a shell or flower, used as a decoration piece on belts, harnesses, etc.

Derringer: a pocket-sized, short-barreled, large-caliber pistol. Named for the US gunsmith Henry Deringer (1786–1868), who designed it.

double eagles: gold coins of the US with a denomination of twenty dollars. They were first minted in 1849. In 1850 regular production began and continued until 1933. Prior to 1850, eagles with a denomination of ten dollars were the largest denomination of US coin. Ten-dollar eagles were produced beginning in 1795 and since the twenty-dollar gold piece had twice the value of the eagle, these coins were designated "double eagles."

dry-gulched: killed; ambushed.

dynamo: a machine by which mechanical energy is changed into electrical energy; a generator.

fanning: 1. waving or slapping the hat against a horse's sides while riding a bucker. Using the hat in this manner serves as a balance and when a rider loses his hat, he is usually not long in following it to the ground. 2. firing a series of shots (from a single-action revolver) by holding the trigger back and successively striking the hammer to the rear with the free hand.

faro: a gambling game played with cards and popular in the American West of the nineteenth century. In faro, the players bet on the order in which the cards will be turned over by the dealer. The cards were kept in a dealing box to keep track of the play.

forty-five or **.45:** a six-shot, single-action, .45-caliber revolver.

G-men: government men; agents of the Federal Bureau of Investigation.

green-gilled: green around the gills; to be pale or sickly in appearance from nervousness or from being frightened.

gunhawk: a wandering gunfighter.

jingle bobs: little pear-shaped pendants hanging loosely from the end of a spur (small spiked wheel attached to the heel of a rider's boot); their sole function is to make music.

Judge Colt: nickname for the single-action (that is, cocked by hand for each shot), six-shot Army model revolver first produced in 1873 by Colt Firearms Company, the armory founded by Samuel Colt (1814–1862). The handgun of the Old West became the instrument of both lawmaker and lawbreaker during the last twenty-five years of the nineteenth century. It soon earned various names, such as "Peacemaker," "Equalizer," and "Judge Colt and his jury of six."

line camp: an outpost cabin, tent or dugout that serves as a base of operations where line riders are housed. *Line riders* are cowboys that follow a ranch's fences or boundaries and maintain order along the borders of a cattleman's property, such as looking after stock, etc.

lobo: 1. gray wolf. 2. wolf; one who is regarded as predatory, greedy and fierce.

locoweed: any of a number of plants widespread in the mountains of the Western US that make livestock act crazy when they eat them.

neck-reined: guided a horse by pressure of the reins against its neck.

owl-hoot: 1. outlaw. 2. owl-hoot trail; an outlaw's way of life.

Piedmont: a type of horse bred in the Piedmont region, an area of land lying between the Appalachian Mountains and the Atlantic coast.

puncher: a hired hand who tends cattle and performs other duties on horseback.

quirt: a riding whip with a short handle and a braided leather lash.

rannies: ranahans; cowboys or top ranch hands.

rowels: the small spiked revolving wheels on the ends of spurs, which are attached to the heels of a rider's boots and used to nudge a horse into going faster.

scatter-gun: a cowboy's name for a shotgun.

Scheherazade: the female narrator of *The Arabian Nights*, who during one thousand and one adventurous nights saved her life by entertaining her husband, the king, with stories.

Sharps: any of several models of firearms devised by Christian Sharps and produced by the Sharps Rifle Company until 1881. The most popular Sharps were "Old Reliable," the cavalry carbine, and the heavy-caliber, single-shot buffalo-hunting rifle. Because of its low muzzle velocity, this gun was said to "fire today, kill tomorrow."

slouch hat: a wide-brimmed felt hat with a chinstrap.

stamping mill: a machine that crushes ore.

Stetson: as the most popular broad-brimmed hat in the West, it became the generic name for hat. John B. Stetson was a master hat maker and founder of the company that has been making Stetsons since 1865. Not only can the Stetson stand up to a terrific amount of beating, the cowboy's hat has more different uses than any other garment he wears. It keeps the sun out of the eyes and off the neck; it serves as an umbrella; it makes a great fan, which sometimes is needed when building a fire or shunting cattle about; the brim serves as a cup to water oneself, or as a bucket to water the horse or put out the fire.

string: a group of animals, especially saddle horses, owned or used by one person.

vaquero: (Spanish) a cowboy or herdsman.

varmints: those people who are obnoxious or make trouble.

war bag: war sack; a cowboy's bag for his personal possessions, plunder, cartridges, etc. Often made of canvas but sometimes just a flour or grain sack and usually tied behind the saddle.

Winchester: an early family of repeating rifles; a single-barreled rifle containing multiple rounds of ammunition. Manufactured by the Winchester Repeating Arms Company, it was widely used in the US during the latter half of the nineteenth century. The 1873 model is often called "the gun that won the West" for its immense popularity at that time, as well as its use in fictional Westerns.

wind devil: a spinning column of air that moves across the landscape and picks up loose dust. It looks like a miniature tornado but is not as powerful.

wrangler: a cowboy who takes care of the saddle horses.

yap: a stupid, crude or loud person.

L. Ron Hubbard
in the Golden Age
of Pulp Fiction

*In writing an adventure story
a writer has to know that he is adventuring
for a lot of people who cannot.
The writer has to take them here and there
about the globe and show them
excitement and love and realism.
As long as that writer is living the part of an
adventurer when he is hammering
the keys, he is succeeding with his story.*

*Adventuring is a state of mind.
If you adventure through life, you have a
good chance to be a success on paper.*

*Adventure doesn't mean globe-trotting,
exactly, and it doesn't mean great deeds.
Adventuring is like art.
You have to live it to make it real.*

— L. RON HUBBARD

L. Ron Hubbard
and American
Pulp Fiction

B ORN March 13, 1911, L. Ron Hubbard lived a life at least as expansive as the stories with which he enthralled a hundred million readers through a fifty-year career.

Originally hailing from Tilden, Nebraska, he spent his formative years in a classically rugged Montana, replete with the cowpunchers, lawmen and desperadoes who would later people his Wild West adventures. And lest anyone imagine those adventures were drawn from vicarious experience, he was not only breaking broncs at a tender age, he was also among the few whites ever admitted into Blackfoot society as a bona fide blood brother. While if only to round out an otherwise rough and tumble youth, his mother was that rarity of her time—a thoroughly educated woman—who introduced her son to the classics of Occidental literature even before his seventh birthday.

But as any dedicated L. Ron Hubbard reader will attest, his world extended far beyond Montana. In point of fact, and as the son of a United States naval officer, by the age of eighteen he had traveled over a quarter of a million miles. Included therein were three Pacific crossings to a then still mysterious Asia, where he ran with the likes of Her British Majesty's agent-in-place

L. Ron Hubbard, left, at Congressional Airport, Washington, DC, 1931, with members of George Washington University flying club.

for North China, and the last in the line of Royal Magicians from the court of Kublai Khan. For the record, L. Ron Hubbard was also among the first Westerners to gain admittance to forbidden Tibetan monasteries below Manchuria, and his photographs of China's Great Wall long graced American geography texts.

Upon his return to the United States and a hasty completion of his interrupted high school education, the young Ron Hubbard entered George Washington University. There, as fans of his aerial adventures may have heard, he earned his wings as a pioneering barnstormer at the dawn of American aviation. He also earned a place in free-flight record books for the longest sustained flight above Chicago. Moreover, as a roving reporter for *Sportsman Pilot* (featuring his first professionally penned articles), he further helped inspire a generation of pilots who would take America to world airpower.

Immediately beyond his sophomore year, Ron embarked on the first of his famed ethnological expeditions, initially to then untrammeled Caribbean shores (descriptions of which would later fill a whole series of West Indies mystery-thrillers). That the Puerto Rican interior would also figure into the future of Ron Hubbard stories was likewise no accident. For in addition to cultural studies of the island, a 1932–33

LRH expedition is rightly remembered as conducting the first complete mineralogical survey of a Puerto Rico under United States jurisdiction.

There was many another adventure along this vein: As a lifetime member of the famed Explorers Club, L. Ron Hubbard charted North Pacific waters with the first shipboard radio direction finder, and so pioneered a long-range navigation system universally employed until the late twentieth century. While not to put too fine an edge on it, he also held a rare Master Mariner's license to pilot any vessel, of any tonnage in any ocean.

Yet lest we stray too far afield, there is an LRH note at this juncture in his saga, and it reads in part:

"I started out writing for the pulps, writing the best I knew, writing for every mag on the stands, slanting as well as I could."

To which one might add: His earliest submissions date from the summer of 1934, and included tales drawn from true-to-life Asian adventures, with characters roughly modeled on British/American intelligence operatives he had known in Shanghai. His early Westerns were similarly peppered with details drawn from personal

Capt. L. Ron Hubbard in Ketchikan, Alaska, 1940, on his Alaskan Radio Experimental Expedition, the first of three voyages conducted under the Explorers Club flag.

experience. Although therein lay a first hard lesson from the often cruel world of the pulps. His first Westerns were soundly rejected as lacking the authenticity of a Max Brand yarn (a particularly frustrating comment given L. Ron Hubbard's Westerns came straight from his Montana homeland, while Max Brand was a mediocre New York poet named Frederick Schiller Faust, who turned out implausible six-shooter tales from the terrace of an Italian villa).

Nevertheless, and needless to say, L. Ron Hubbard persevered and soon earned a reputation as among the most publishable names in pulp fiction, with a ninety percent placement rate of first-draft manuscripts. He was also among the most prolific, averaging between seventy and a hundred thousand words a month. Hence the rumors that L. Ron Hubbard had redesigned a typewriter for faster keyboard action and pounded out manuscripts on a continuous roll of butcher paper to save the precious seconds it took to insert a single sheet of paper into manual typewriters of the day.

That all L. Ron Hubbard stories did not run beneath said byline is yet another aspect of pulp fiction lore. That is, as publishers periodically rejected manuscripts from top-drawer authors if only to avoid paying top dollar, L. Ron Hubbard and company just as frequently replied with submissions under various pseudonyms. In Ron's case, the list

A MAN OF MANY NAMES

Between 1934 and 1950, L. Ron Hubbard authored more than fifteen million words of fiction in more than two hundred classic publications. To supply his fans and editors with stories across an array of genres and pulp titles, he adopted fifteen pseudonyms in addition to his already renowned L. Ron Hubbard byline.

Winchester Remington Colt
Lt. Jonathan Daly
Capt. Charles Gordon
Capt. L. Ron Hubbard
Bernard Hubbel
Michael Keith
Rene Lafayette
Legionnaire 148
Legionnaire 14830
Ken Martin
Scott Morgan
Lt. Scott Morgan
Kurt von Rachen
Barry Randolph
Capt. Humbert Reynolds

included: Rene Lafayette, Captain Charles Gordon, Lt. Scott Morgan and the notorious Kurt von Rachen—supposedly on the lam for a murder rap, while hammering out two-fisted prose in Argentina. The point: While L. Ron Hubbard as Ken Martin spun stories of Southeast Asian intrigue, LRH as Barry Randolph authored tales of

L. Ron Hubbard, circa 1930, at the outset of a literary career that would finally span half a century.

romance on the Western range—which, stretching between a dozen genres is how he came to stand among the two hundred elite authors providing close to a million tales through the glory days of American Pulp Fiction.

In evidence of exactly that, by 1936 L. Ron Hubbard was literally leading pulp fiction's elite as president of New York's American Fiction Guild. Members included a veritable pulp hall of fame: Lester "Doc Savage" Dent, Walter "The Shadow" Gibson, and the legendary Dashiell Hammett—to cite but a few.

Also in evidence of just where L. Ron Hubbard stood within his first two years on the American pulp circuit: By the spring of 1937, he was ensconced in Hollywood, adopting a Caribbean thriller for Columbia Pictures, remembered today as *The Secret of Treasure Island*. Comprising fifteen thirty-minute episodes, the L. Ron Hubbard screenplay led to the most profitable matinée serial in Hollywood history. In accord with Hollywood culture, he was thereafter continually called

The 1937 Secret of Treasure Island, a fifteen-episode serial adapted for the screen by L. Ron Hubbard from his novel, Murder at Pirate Castle.

upon to rewrite/doctor scripts—most famously for long-time friend and fellow adventurer Clark Gable.

In the interim—and herein lies another distinctive chapter of the L. Ron Hubbard story—he continually worked to open Pulp Kingdom gates to up-and-coming authors. Or, for that matter, anyone who wished to write. It was a fairly unconventional stance, as markets were already thin and competition razor sharp. But the fact remains, it was an L. Ron Hubbard hallmark that he vehemently lobbied on behalf of young authors—regularly supplying instructional articles to trade journals, guest-lecturing to short story classes at George Washington University and Harvard, and even founding his own creative writing competition. It was established in 1940, dubbed the Golden Pen, and guaranteed winners both New York representation and publication in *Argosy*.

But it was John W. Campbell Jr.'s *Astounding Science Fiction* that finally proved the most memorable LRH vehicle. While every fan of L. Ron Hubbard's galactic epics undoubtedly knows the story, it nonetheless bears repeating: By late 1938, the pulp publishing magnate of Street & Smith was determined to revamp *Astounding Science Fiction* for broader readership. In particular, senior editorial director F. Orlin Tremaine called for stories with a stronger *human element*. When acting editor John W. Campbell balked, preferring his spaceship-driven tales,

Tremaine enlisted Hubbard. Hubbard, in turn, replied with the genre's first truly *character-driven* works, wherein heroes are pitted not against bug-eyed monsters but the mystery and majesty of deep space itself—and thus was launched the Golden Age of Science Fiction.

The names alone are enough to quicken the pulse of any science fiction aficionado, including LRH friend and protégé, Robert Heinlein, Isaac Asimov, A. E. van Vogt and Ray Bradbury. Moreover, when coupled with LRH stories of fantasy, we further come to what's rightly been described as the foundation of every modern tale of horror: L. Ron Hubbard's immortal *Fear.* It was rightly proclaimed by Stephen King as one of the very few works to genuinely warrant that overworked term "classic"—as in: *"This is a classic tale of creeping, surreal menace and horror. . . . This is one of the really, really good ones."*

L. Ron Hubbard, 1948, among fellow science fiction luminaries at the World Science Fiction Convention in Toronto.

To accommodate the greater body of L. Ron Hubbard fantasies, Street & Smith inaugurated *Unknown*—a classic pulp if there ever was one, and wherein readers were soon thrilling to the likes of *Typewriter in the Sky* and *Slaves of Sleep* of which Frederik Pohl would declare: *"There are bits and pieces from Ron's work that became part of the language in ways that very few other writers managed."*

And, indeed, at J. W. Campbell Jr.'s insistence, Ron was regularly drawing on themes from the Arabian Nights and so introducing readers to a world of genies, jinn, Aladdin and Sinbad—all of which, of course, continue to float through cultural mythology to this day.

At least as influential in terms of post-apocalypse stories was L. Ron Hubbard's 1940 *Final Blackout*. Generally acclaimed as the finest anti-war novel of the decade and among the ten best works of the genre ever authored—here, too, was a tale that would live on in ways few other writers

imagined. Hence, the later Robert Heinlein verdict: "Final Blackout *is as perfect a piece of science fiction as has ever been written.*"

Like many another who both lived and wrote American pulp adventure, the war proved a tragic end to Ron's sojourn in the pulps. He served with distinction in four theaters and was highly decorated for commanding corvettes in the North Pacific. He was also grievously wounded in combat, lost many a close friend and colleague and thus resolved to say farewell to pulp fiction and devote himself to what it had supported these many years—namely, his serious research.

Portland, Oregon, 1943; L. Ron Hubbard captain of the US Navy subchaser PC 815.

But in no way was the LRH literary saga at an end, for as he wrote some thirty years later, in 1980:

"Recently there came a period when I had little to do. This was novel in a life so crammed with busy years, and I decided to amuse myself by writing a novel that was pure science fiction."

That work was *Battlefield Earth: A Saga of the Year 3000.* It was an immediate *New York Times* bestseller and, in fact, the first international science fiction blockbuster in decades. It was not, however, L. Ron Hubbard's magnum opus, as that distinction is generally reserved for his next and final work: The 1.2 million word *Mission Earth.*

> **Final Blackout**
> *is as perfect a piece of science fiction as has ever been written.*
>
> —Robert Heinlein

How he managed those 1.2 million words in just over twelve months is yet another piece of the L. Ron Hubbard legend. But the fact remains, he did indeed author a ten-volume *dekalogy* that lives in publishing history for the fact that each and every volume of the series was also a *New York Times* bestseller.

Moreover, as subsequent generations discovered L. Ron Hubbard through republished works and novelizations of his screenplays, the mere fact of his name on a cover signaled an international bestseller. . . . Until, to date, sales of his works exceed hundreds of millions, and he otherwise remains among the most enduring and widely read authors in literary history. Although as a final word on the tales of L. Ron Hubbard, perhaps it's enough to simply reiterate what editors told readers in the glory days of American Pulp Fiction:

He writes the way he does, brothers, because he's been there, seen it and done it!

THE STORIES FROM THE GOLDEN AGE

Your ticket to adventure starts here with the Stories from
the Golden Age collection by master storyteller L. Ron Hubbard.
These gripping tales are set in a kaleidoscope of exotic locales and brim
with fascinating characters, including some of the
most vile villains, dangerous dames and brazen heroes
you'll ever get to meet.

The entire collection of over one hundred and fifty stories is being
released in a series of eighty books and audiobooks.
For an up-to-date listing of available titles,
go to www.goldenagestories.com.

AIR ADVENTURE

<table>
<tr><td>Arctic Wings</td><td>Man-Killers of the Air</td></tr>
<tr><td>The Battling Pilot</td><td>On Blazing Wings</td></tr>
<tr><td>Boomerang Bomber</td><td>Red Death Over China</td></tr>
<tr><td>The Crate Killer</td><td>Sabotage in the Sky</td></tr>
<tr><td>The Dive Bomber</td><td>Sky Birds Dare!</td></tr>
<tr><td>Forbidden Gold</td><td>The Sky-Crasher</td></tr>
<tr><td>Hurtling Wings</td><td>Trouble on His Wings</td></tr>
<tr><td>The Lieutenant Takes the Sky</td><td>Wings Over Ethiopia</td></tr>
</table>

FAR-FLUNG ADVENTURE

The Adventure of "X"   *Hurricane*
All Frontiers Are Jealous   *The Iron Duke*
The Barbarians   *Machine Gun 21,000*
The Black Sultan   *Medals for Mahoney*
Black Towers to Danger   *Price of a Hat*
The Bold Dare All   *Red Sand*
Buckley Plays a Hunch   *The Sky Devil*
The Cossack   *The Small Boss of Nunaloha*
Destiny's Drum   *The Squad That Never Came Back*
Escape for Three   *Starch and Stripes*
Fifty-Fifty O'Brien   *Tomb of the Ten Thousand Dead*
The Headhunters   *Trick Soldier*
Hell's Legionnaire   *While Bugles Blow!*
He Walked to War   *Yukon Madness*
Hostage to Death

SEA ADVENTURE

Cargo of Coffins   *The Phantom Patrol*
The Drowned City   *Sea Fangs*
False Cargo   *Submarine*
Grounded   *Twenty Fathoms Down*
Loot of the Shanung   *Under the Black Ensign*
Mister Tidwell, Gunner

TALES FROM THE ORIENT

The Devil—With Wings *Pearl Pirate*
The Falcon Killer *The Red Dragon*
Five Mex for a Million *Spy Killer*
Golden Hell *Tah*
The Green God *The Trail of the Red Diamonds*
Hurricane's Roar *Wind-Gone-Mad*
Inky Odds *Yellow Loot*
Orders Is Orders

MYSTERY

The Blow Torch Murder *The Grease Spot*
Brass Keys to Murder *Killer Ape*
Calling Squad Cars! *Killer's Law*
The Carnival of Death *The Mad Dog Murder*
The Chee-Chalker *Mouthpiece*
Dead Men Kill *Murder Afloat*
The Death Flyer *The Slickers*
Flame City *They Killed Him Dead*

127

FANTASY

SCIENCE FICTION

WESTERN

129

JOIN THE PULP REVIVAL
America in the 1930s and 40s

Pulp fiction was in its heyday and 30 million readers were regularly riveted by the larger-than-life tales of master storyteller L. Ron Hubbard. For this was pulp fiction's golden age, when the writing was raw and every page packed a walloping punch.

That magic can now be yours. An evocative world of nefarious villains, exotic intrigues, courageous heroes and heroines—a world that today's cinema has barely tapped for tales of adventure and swashbucklers.

Enroll today in the Stories from the Golden Age Club and begin receiving your monthly feature edition selected from more than 150 stories in the collection.

You may choose to enjoy them as either a paperback or audiobook for the special membership price of $9.95 each month along with FREE shipping and handling.

CALL TOLL-FREE: 1-877-8GALAXY
(1-877-842-5299) OR GO ONLINE TO
www.goldenagestories.com
AND BECOME PART OF THE PULP REVIVAL!